She turned at the sound o̶f̶ ̶.̶.̶.̶.̶ The children. Of course. ̶T̶h̶e̶ ̶c̶h̶i̶l̶d̶r̶e̶n̶. She looked at them encircling the bed and remembered that they were not her children but the school's. The kid fix she sought when she couldn't have her own.

The euphoria of a moment ago collapsed, and with it came the bitter disappointment that always returned to take hold of her when she allowed herself to think about her marriage, her divorce, all the things she wanted that she'd never have.

She gazed into dark-lashed hazel eyes set in a handsome face crowned with short dark brown hair.

She put her fingertips to her mouth, recalling those nicely shaped lips on hers and the renewal she'd believed he'd brought to her life.

But he wasn't Ben, her former husband. He was a stranger. And she didn't care what he was doing here, or why she was in bed with the children gathered around her.

The only thing that mattered was that he'd led her to believe the pain was over and life was going to begin again.

It wasn't, though. And it was all his fault.

She raised a hand and slapped him as hard as she could.

Dear Reader,

Don't you love a man who knows what to say? "Honey, that tofu-eggplant-pasta casserole was delicious." "No, harem pants do not make you look fat." "I know the children are a handful, but you make motherhood look easy."

Okay, I'm fantasizing. Most men think honesty is more important than hurt feelings. Many seasoned husbands do catch on eventually, but not before their wives learn to deal with bruised egos. And it's not as though we don't know the truth; it's just that we're hoping our men love us enough to see the capable, slender, clever image we want to project.

In *Man with a Message*, Cameron Trent is a hero filled with love and compassion for Mariah Mercer, who wants no part of him. Though she continually puts herself at odds with him, he always seems to know what to say to her, how to support and encourage her, and help her make her dreams come true. Maybe we should have him cloned.

Sit back and put your feet up. And you might want to get some chocolate. Cam and Mariah have a rocky road to romance.

All my best!

Muriel Jensen
P.O. Box 1168
Astoria, Oregon 97103

Man with a Message

Muriel Jensen

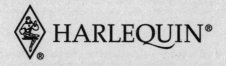

HARLEQUIN®

TORONTO • NEW YORK • LONDON
AMSTERDAM • PARIS • SYDNEY • HAMBURG
STOCKHOLM • ATHENS • TOKYO • MILAN • MADRID
PRAGUE • WARSAW • BUDAPEST • AUCKLAND

ISBN 0-373-71056-9

MAN WITH A MESSAGE

Copyright © 2002 by Muriel Jensen.

This edition published by arrangement with Harlequin Books S.A.

® and TM are trademarks of the publisher. Trademarks indicated with ® are registered in the United States Patent and Trademark Office, the Canadian Trade Marks Office and in other countries.

Visit us at www.eHarlequin.com

Printed in U.S.A.

Man with a Message

CHAPTER ONE

CAMERON TRENT WALKED around the Maple Hill Common in the waning light of a late-May evening. Fred, his seven-month-old black Labrador, investigated bushes and wildflowers at the other end of a retractable leash.

The dog looked back at him, eyes bright, tongue lolling; he was out and about after sleeping in the truck for three hours while Cam installed an old ball-and-claw bathtub in a Georgian mansion near the lake.

Life is good, Fred's expression said.

Cam had to agree.

Moving from San Francisco to Maple Hill, Massachusetts, situated on the edge of the Berkshires, had been an inspired idea. He and his brother and sister had spent a couple of weeks here as children every summer with their grandparents. It was the only time he could pick out of his childhood when he'd felt happy and safe.

As Cam wandered after Fred, he took in the colonial charm of the scene. A bronze Minuteman, his woman at his side, dominated the square. A colonial flag and a fifty-star flag were just being lowered for the night as Cam walked by. During working hours, the shops and businesses built around the green-lawned square bustled with activity, very much as they had two hundred years ago.

Many of the houses in Maple Hill were Classic Georgian, with its heroic columns, or the simpler salt-box style, with its long, sloping roof in the rear. In Yankee tradition, small boats hung from the ceilings of some porches, and many houses bore historic plaques explaining their history. And Amherst, where he was earning his master's in business administration was a mere hour away.

He had everything he needed right here. Well almost. He missed his brother, Josh, but he was a chef in a Los Angeles restaurant and raising his wife's four boys, and it was good to know he was happy.

Whitcomb's Wonders, the agency of tradesmen Cam worked for as a plumber, had become his family. They were a cheerful, striving group of men who enjoyed working part-time for the company because it allowed them to pursue other endeavors—raise their children, go to school.

Fred came running back to Cam, his head held high so that he could hold on to a giant branch that protruded at least two feet out of each side of his mouth. His tail wagged furiously.

They were in the middle of a serious tug-of-war

over the branch when Cam's cell phone rang. Cam tossed the branch, then answered.

"Mariah Mercer from the Manor says they're sinking!" Addy Whitcomb told him urgently. "A pipe in the bathroom burst."

Cam reeled in the dog, who'd just headed off to chase the branch. Repairing the Maple Hill Manor School was a lucrative job for Whitcomb's Wonders. One of the oldest buildings around, it was a plumbing and wiring disaster. They'd just been contracted to replumb the kitchen in the main building as part of a remodeling project.

"The bathroom in the main building?" he asked.

"No, the dorm. You know, the old carriage house."

"Okay. I'm in town. I'll be there in about ten minutes."

"I'll call and tell her. And just to reward you, Cam, I'll find you a really wonderful girl."

"No favors necessary, Addy." Addy was Hank Whitcomb's mother. Whitcomb's Wonders was Hank's brainchild, and the men who staffed it provided the source for much of Addy's Cupid work.

"But I want to!"

"No. Got to go, Addy."

Fred was disappointed at no more play but enjoyed the sprint across the common toward the truck. Cam let him into the passenger side, then ran around to climb in behind the wheel. The truck's tires peeled away with a squeal as he headed for the Manor. He'd outfitted his somewhat decrepit old truck to hold his tools and supplies so he was always ready to report to a job.

He tried to imagine what could have caused a pipe to burst. Pipes often froze and broke in the winter, but this was spring. And the Lightfoot sisters, who ran the school, had told him that they'd renewed the carriage house plumbing about ten years ago.

He knew that only a small number of children still boarded at the school, and did so only because of long relationships with the Lightfoot sisters, who'd taken over running the school from their mother in the fifties, after she'd taken it over from her mother, and so on all the way back to pre-Civil War days.

Letitia and Lavinia Lightfoot, who both charmed and intimidated the crew working on the renovation, were in their late seventies and still took pride in the bastion of civility they managed in a world they considered both fascinating and mad.

Cam refocused his attention on a series of curves, then exited onto Manor Road, which led through a thick oak, maple and pine woods to a clearing where the school stood, one of the finest examples of Georgian architecture in western Massachusetts. He turned left toward the carriage house, instead of right toward the main building.

It was dark now and all he could see of the carriage house, a replica of the main building but smaller, were its white columns, caught in the floodlights that illuminated the small parking area in the front. He pulled up beside a van, gave Fred a dog biscuit and spread his blanket on the seat. "Relax, buddy," he said, patting the dog's head. "I don't know how long I'll be."

Fred, just happy for the attention, cooperated.

Cam grabbed his basic tool kit and went to knock on the front door. He could hear a great commotion on the other side—children shouting, feet hurrying.

The door opened with a jerk and a little blond girl wearing neon-orange pajamas stood there, pale and breathing heavily. Behind her children ran up and down the stairs with towels and buckets. He heard a boy yelling from upstairs, "Turn the cutoff...it looks like a faucet!"

A younger male voice yelled back, "I don't see it! I don't see it!" he said again.

The little blond girl turned to shout up the stairs, "He's here!"

"Tell him to hurry!" the boy replied.

Cam experienced a weird sense of unreality, as if he'd blundered into a world occupied only by children. Not one adult was in evidence.

"Come on!" The little blonde grabbed his wrist and pulled him inside.

He allowed her to tow him up the stairway, its carpeting soggy. There was water everywhere, inches of it in the narrow upstairs hall.

Water rushed from the bathroom through a large hole in a pipe visible because of the broken tiles in the shower stall.

"Hey!"

The boy's voice made him look down. He saw a woman lying on her back, apparently unconscious, the boy's arm keeping her head out of the water. Her face was familiar. Cam had seen her around the school while scoping out the kitchen in the main building.

He dropped his tool kit on a sink and fell to his knees.

"You're not the ambulance guy?" the boy asked. He was about ten, his dark eyes panicky, his face ashen.

"No, I'm the plumber," Cam replied, putting two fingers to the pulse at the woman's throat. He couldn't detect one, but then, he could never find one in himself, either. "What happened?"

The boy appeared close to tears. "I busted the pipe looking for gold. She came in, slipped on a towel in the water and fell and hit her head. I'm not supposed to move her, right? I mean, she could have broken something."

Gold? Cam didn't even take the time to try to figure out what that meant. He did a cursory exploration of arms and legs and detected nothing out of place. She didn't seem to be bleeding. He decided that getting her out of the water took precedence over maybe causing her further injury.

"Is there a dry bed anywhere?" He slipped his arms under her and lifted her. She was small and fragile. Water streamed from her all over him as he stepped back to let the boy lead the way.

"In here!" The boy beckoned him into a room two doors off the bathroom. Cam noticed absently that the doors had hand-painted signs with kids' names on them.

A pack of children followed them and gathered around the bed as Cam lay the woman down.

She looked younger up close than he'd thought. Her dark hair, now drenched, was pulled back into a tight knot, and she wore a silky, long-sleeved blouse, through which he could see her lacy bra. A long blue cotton skirt lay clumped around her, also heavy with water. She'd struck him as stiff and matronly when he'd seen her at the school. How different his impression of her now.

He wrapped the coverlet around her.

He leaned close to tell if she was breathing. He felt no air against his cheek, heard no sound. Where was the ambulance? He'd taken a CPR course a few years ago, but he couldn't remember it now. So many pumps, so many breaths.

"She's gonna die!" one of the little girls said tearfully.

"No, she won't!" the boy said.

"She won't!" another boy repeated.

"She won't!"

Cam glanced up, wondering why he kept hearing double, then realized he was seeing double, too. Twins.

The woman made a scary, choking sound and the children cried out in unison.

Knowing he had to do something, he shooed the children aside, leaned over the woman, pinched her nose and placed his mouth over hers.

She was cold and still in his arms, like a marble statue.

He blew air into her mouth, raised his head to see if it was having an effect. When he couldn't detect one, he covered her mouth again and breathed into it. After several more breaths, a curious thing happened. He felt the first infinitesimal sign of life as a small, almost sinuous exhalation swelled the breasts under his chest.

Disbelieving, he breathed into her again, and that same subtle ripple occurred in the lips under his.

He put a hand to her ribs, feeling for an intake of breath, even as he gave her another one of his.

When he felt the probing tip of a tongue in his mouth, he thought he was hallucinating—giving her too much of his air, not keeping enough for himself.

Then her lips moved under his, and before he could raise his head in surprise, one of her hands went into his hair in a caress that paralyzed him momentarily into helplessness.

As he hovered above her in shock, her body arched up to his and she expelled a little moan. ''Ben,'' she murmured against his lips.

For an instant, everything in him rose to the challenge. Yes! This was what life was supposed to be about! Man and woman entangled, seeking solace and pleasure in each other, their bodies a mutual haven. He'd have given a lot at that instant to be the Ben she sighed for.

Then reality reclaimed him and he sat up abruptly, the children all staring, not sure what they'd seen.

His heart was beating hard, then his brain snapped to attention. *This kind of thing won't work for you,* it told him. *You have a past. Allison had thought it wouldn't matter, but eventually it did. You're starting over, but you'll only get half the dream....*

The woman opened deep brown eyes, and after a moment of searching the room, a puzzled line between her brows, she focused on him. A small smile of what appeared to be—he wasn't sure...surprise? delight?—curved her pale lips.

No one had ever looked at him that way—as if he represented home at the end of a long journey. He still leaned over her, a hand on the mattress on either side of her, unable to move or speak.

MARIAH SURFACED FROM her chilled dream to find that the last year had all been some kind of terrible

misunderstanding. Ben was back the way she remembered him at their wedding—the loving, solid
partner around whom she'd centered her hopes,
rather than the angry and confused man he'd become after she'd lost four babies and refused to try
again to get pregnant.

Then his mouth had been hard and condemning.
Now it was pliant and…life giving.

But why were they surrounded by children?
They'd never be able to have their own. And he
hadn't wanted to consider adoption—

"Mariah?"

She turned at the sound of her name and focused
on…on Ashley? Of course. Ashley. She looked at
the children circling the bed and remembered that
they were not her children, but the Manor's. The kid
fix she'd sought when she couldn't have her own.

The euphoria of a moment ago collapsed, and
with it came the bitter disappointment that always
returned to take hold of her when she allowed herself to think about her marriage, her divorce, all the
things she wanted that she'd never have.

She gazed into dark-lashed hazel eyes set in a
handsome face crowned with very short dark brown
hair.

She put her fingertips to her mouth, recalling
those nicely shaped lips on hers and the renewal
she'd thought he'd brought to her life.

But he wasn't Ben. He was a stranger. And she didn't care what he was doing here or why she was in bed with the children gathered around her.

The only thing that mattered was that he'd led her to believe the pain was over and life was going to begin again.

It wasn't, though. And it was all his fault.

She raised a hand and slapped him as hard as she could.

CHAPTER TWO

"No, MARIAH!" BRIAN, standing beside the stranger, caught her wrist. "He saved your life! I broke the water pipe—remember?—and you slipped on the towel and fell and hit your head. He carried you in here. He didn't kiss you. He gave you artificial...you know."

"Resuscitation," Ashley said knowledgeably. "But I think you kissed him."

"Yeah," Jessica said. "I saw it."

"Me, too," Peter confirmed.

"Me, too," Philip chimed in.

Mariah groaned and put her hands to her face. If she didn't get herself together soon, she had no hope for her future. Once the school found out she was French-kissing strange men in front of the children, she'd have to take the job her sister, Parker, had offered her—working in her massage studio in the basement of city hall. Then she'd never get to Europe.

Mariah felt movement on the bed, and when she lowered her hands, she saw that the stranger was gone.

Brian took off after him, calling over his shoulder, "We're going to cut off the water!"

The screeching of a siren could be heard outside.

"I'll let the ambulance men in," Ashley shouted as she left the room.

The children stood back and Mariah sat up. She was horrified that an ambulance had been called.

"I don't think you're supposed to get up," Jessica said worriedly, sitting beside her.

Mariah's intention was to tell her that she was fine, but she realized suddenly that she wasn't. Her head ached abominably, and suddenly everything around her was wobbling.

Two men in white shirts with some kind of insignia on them burst into the room. One cupped her head gently with his hand and leaned her back into the pillows. "What's your name, ma'am?" he asked.

"Mariah," she replied weakly.

"I understand you've had a fall."

That's an understatement, she thought as she battled nausea. The Fall of Mariah Mercer could be a play in three acts.

WITH THE LITTLE BOY NAMED Brian shining a flashlight into the dark corners of the basement, Cam found the cutoff and turned it off. When he raced back upstairs, Brian at his heels, the paramedics were putting a protesting Mariah on a gurney.

"I cannot leave the children!" she insisted. "There are eight children under ten years of age..."

"We're here, dear. We're here." The Lightfoot sisters appeared in the hallway, looking as though they'd just stepped out of a family portrait, circa 1930-something. They wore their usual long black dresses with lace collars. Letitia, the elder sister, had a small gold watch attached to her generous bosom. Lavinia, younger and smaller, had a sprig of silk violets pinned at the waist of her dress. Cam had had several meetings with them to discuss the kitchen renovation, and he'd found them surprisingly sharp in business, considering their vintage clothing and their charmingly old-fashioned approach to education.

"Ashley called us." Letitia put an arm around the girl's shoulders. "You gentlemen take good care of Mariah!" she admonished the paramedics, who were heading for the stairs. "I know your mother, Matthew Collingwood. I'll have a word with her if Mariah isn't returned to us in perfect health."

The paramedic pushing the gurney cast a smile over his shoulder. "Don't worry, Miss Letty. She'll be fine. Watch the stairs, Charlie."

"Well, now!" The sisters shooed the children toward the back of the house. "While Miss Lavinia calls the janitorial service to clean up the water, we're going to camp here. Where are the sleeping bags from our hiking trip during spring break?"

Jessica and her sisters pulled down the attic stairs and fought over who would climb up to get them.

Letty tried to enlist Brian's help, but he turned to Cam. "I could help you," he whispered pleadingly.

"Ah...I'm sort of using him as my assistant," Cam said. "Is it all right if I keep him for another hour or so?"

Letitia appeared concerned. "If you keep a close eye on him. He's eager to help and sometimes..." She was obviously searching for a diplomatic explanation.

Cam understood. "He'll be right beside me at all times."

Brian gave him a grateful look.

"All right, then," Letitia replied. "Brian, I'm counting on you to do exactly as you're told."

"Yes, ma'am," he promised.

"Good." Cam put a hand on the boy's shoulder. "For safety's sake, I'm going to turn off the power. With water everywhere, I don't want anyone touching light switches, even where it's dry."

"Right."

He was about to ask Miss Letty if she had a flashlight to lead the children in the dark house, when she shouted up the attic stairs, "Jessie, bring the camp lanterns down with you, too!"

Cam grabbed the flashlight from his tool kit and, with Brian glued to his side, hurried back downstairs to shut down the power. He handed Brian the flashlight.

"This is so cool!" Brian said. "Nothing exciting ever happens around here." Then apparently he realized what he'd said and looked sheepish. "I mean, I know it's all my fault and it's caused everybody a lot of trouble. And you probably charge a whole lot."

"Yeah, I do." With all the circuit breakers flipped, Cam and Brian stood in darkness except for the glow from the flashlight. "And the guys who have to clean up the water cost a bundle, too."

Brian sighed. "I was going to take everybody to Disneyland for summer vacation if I found the gold."

Cam turned him toward the stairs and let him lead the way with the light. "You mentioned that before. What gold are you talking about?"

The boy told him a story about a Confederate spy trying to escape to the South with a satchel full of gold. "He was in this building when he was shot, and the Yankees and the Lightfoots who owned the Manor then found the satchel, but not the gold. Everybody knows the story."

"I've never heard it."

"Mr. Groman told me. He teaches here, you know. Some rebel soldier stole it off a train and hid out with it in the carriage house. When they tiled the bathroom floor, they covered up the blood!"

The kid had a flair for theatrics, Cam thought, and was probably destined for a career in front of a camera.

They climbed the stairs, Brian holding the light to his side for Cam's benefit. "But if it hasn't been found in a hundred and fifty years…"

"A hundred and thirty-seven," Brian corrected him.

"A hundred and thirty-seven," Cam said obligingly, "why did you suddenly think you'd find it in the bathroom wall?"

They'd reached the main level. Brian waited while Cam closed and locked the basement door. "Because I thought about it. They didn't find it when they tore up the floor to put down new stuff, so where else could it be?"

"Somewhere in the attic?"

"Looked there."

"And you probably checked the basement."

"A couple of times."

"Maybe this spy had an accomplice and passed it on or something."

Brian frowned. "I guess that could be. But that's not in the story."

They made their way carefully toward the stairway to the second floor. "There's probably an old newspaper account of the incident," Cam suggested. "In the library. Old newspapers are scanned into the computer. Or maybe they could help you at the *Mirror*."

Brian grinned in the near darkness as they went up the stairs side by side. "Maybe Mariah will take me," he said hopefully. Then suddenly his expression turned doubtful. "If she can forget that I almost killed her."

Cam ran a knuckle down his own cheek, remembering her slap, and patted Brian's shoulder. "I don't think she was as near death as it seemed. Apologize first, then ask her."

In the bathroom once again, Cam tore out more tiles to get at the pipe connection while Brian held the flashlight for him.

"About your plans for the gold," he said. "Aren't you all going home for the summer?"

"Yeah, but Ashley doesn't have parents, you know. She just has a guardian and he's pretty old. She never gets to stay home with him. He sends her on trips with people she doesn't know and she hates it. They think she doesn't know, but he's going to die pretty soon."

When Cam looked down at him, not sure what to say to that, Brian added with a shrug, "We hear the teachers talking. She's going to have to go live with somebody else. My mom's a movie star."

Cam had difficulty focusing on the plumbing and the conversation. "No kidding?"

"No. She's very pretty, but she's always on a movie set somewhere far away and I stay with the housekeeper. Pete and Repeat's mom and dad are stunt people and they're working with my mom in a movie right now. In Mongolia."

"Pete and *Repeat?*"

"The twins."

"Ah."

"They're really Pete and Philip, but their dad calls 'em 'Pete and Repeat.' Now everyone does. Their dad jumps off cliffs and out of airplanes and over waterfalls. Their mom once jumped out of a building on fire! I mean *she* was on fire. 'Course, the building probably was, too, or she wouldn't have been. She had a special suit on so she wouldn't get burned. Cool, huh?"

"I'm not sure I'd want to be on fire, even in a special suit."

"Jessie and her sisters' mom wants to take them to New York with her to visit a friend of hers. So they don't want to go home for the summer, either."

"Jessie and her sisters are those four dark-haired little girls who all look alike?"

"Yeah, only they get smaller and smaller. Like those toy things that fit into each other. You know?"

Cam had to grin at him. The kid had such an interesting little mind. "Yeah, I know. But what's wrong with meeting their mom's friend? New York's a very exciting place."

"He's a guy."

"Well, so are we. Is that bad?"

Brian seemed to like being considered a guy. Cam had to remind him to hold up the light.

"It's because their mom likes him and they don't want another dad."

"What happened to the first one?"

"He and their mom got divorced."

"Ah. That's too bad."

There was a moment's silence, then Brian announced, "I don't have one."

"What? A father?"

"Yeah. I never had one. And he didn't die and my mom's not divorced. I mean, he's probably somewhere, but he's not my dad."

Cam nodded empathetically, catching the significance of that detail from the boy's tone of voice. Brian wanted to adjust to that fact but still hadn't.

"I had a father," Cam said, carefully applying pressure to the wrench. "But he was drunk a lot and most of the time it was like I didn't have one."

"Did he beat you up?"

"No. Most of the time he didn't remember I was there."

"Did you have a cool mom?"

Cam wasn't sure how far to carry this empathy. He wanted Brian to know he wasn't alone in an unfair world, but he wasn't sure what it would serve to tell Brian it could get worse than he knew.

"No," he replied simply. "She was gone most of the time."

His mother had been out of jail only three weeks when she and a male friend had been picked up for armed robbery. Cam and his siblings had had the misfortune of being with her at home at the time, their father passed out on the sofa, beer cans and a bottle of whiskey beside him.

With their mother going to jail and their father

deemed unfit to raise them, he and his siblings had been placed in foster care. He'd argued zealously that he'd taken care of himself and his brother and sister most of his life—that all the other times his mother had gone to jail his father had also turned up drunk and Cam was the one who had cooked and done laundry and gotten himself, Josh and Barbara off to school.

No one had cared about that. Their grandfather had died, their grandmother was in a nursing home and the three Trent children were placed together in foster care with a middle-aged couple who lived in the heart of the city.

Deprived of the choice of how to live his life, Cam became bent on destroying it. Fortunately, he'd been caught with a few of his friends holding up a restaurant while the owner was closing. A few months in juvenile hall had turned him around. Foster care seemed like heaven after that.

"My mom's always in another country 'cause of the acting thing," Brian said. "What'd yours do?"

"Ah…" He had to think to recollect what had identified her place in his life besides the drugs and the jail time. "She worked in a furniture factory."

"She drink, too?"

Cam was so surprised by the question that he stopped what he was doing to focus on the boy.

Brian shrugged. "It's a statistic that a lot of people who drink do it with a husband or wife or boyfriend."

Cam was sure that was true but he wondered how the boy knew. "Who told you that?"

"My mom's in rehab a lot." It seemed to be something he had accepted. "It happened one time in the summer, and the housekeeper took me to visit her. We had to sit in at this meeting about families of substance abusers."

Cam had never known the politically correct term because there'd been no one to take him to meetings.

"Come on," he said. "We're going out to the truck. Remember to keep your hands off the switches."

"We going to the shop or something?" Brian asked excitedly, taking the lead with the flashlight.

"No. I've got pipe in the truck."

They reached the third stair from the bottom and Brian leaped down, the carpet squishing as he landed. "So, is it cool to be a plumber?"

Cam could feel his soaked shoes and socks and jeans and smiled into the darkness. "Oh, it's way cool."

CHAPTER THREE

MARIAH'S SISTER WAS BESIDE herself with worry when she arrived at the emergency room. "Oh, my God!" she exclaimed, swiping a white curtain aside to come to Mariah's side. "Are you all right?"

Mariah sat up, fine except for pain in the bump at the back of her head. She explained briefly about Brian's search for gold and the resulting deluge.

Parker shook her head sympathetically. "That kid's going to blow up the world one day."

Mariah sighed. "He's the sweetest boy, but I'm going to have to build a cage around him for the safety of the other children."

"And you. Do you have a concussion?"

"Just a mild one. The doctor's worried, though, because I passed out."

"You passed *out?* Did you stop breathing?"

"I'm not sure. I dreamed…" She put a hand to her throat as she recalled a drowning sensation, as if she was falling into a well, unable to draw in air. "Someone gave me…mouth-to-mouth," she explained, remembering with abrupt clarity her grave disappointment when the face bent over her wasn't Ben's but that of some stranger's.

Some stranger she'd just kissed with the desperate need she'd never revealed to anyone.

Someone whose eyes said that he'd felt that need in her.

Bitter disappointment over the loss of her babies, the loss of her marriage, the loss of her mask of stoic courage, had all required that she punch his lights out.

"Oh, God!" She put a hand to her face and groaned.

"Nurse!" Parker shouted.

"Sh!" Mariah lowered her hand and placed it over Parker's mouth. "I'm fine! I just…just remembered something."

"What? You looked as though you were going to slide right off onto the floor."

"I…I was just thinking about the cleanup at the dorm." Mariah frowned apologetically. "I'm sorry, Parker, but the doctor won't let me go home tonight if there isn't someone to watch me. Can you take me home with you, just for tonight?"

"Of course! It'll be fun. I just made carrot cookies."

Mariah tried to look pleased at that. As much as she loved her sister, she had very different opinions about what defined a comfortable environment. Parker was a naturalist, earth-mother sort of woman;

Mariah's approach to life was much more traditional.

Parker had a heart of gold, but her sofa was a red vinyl banquette from a Japanese restaurant, and two hammocks suspended from the ceiling constituted her bedroom.

All of a sudden Parker smiled. "Who gave you mouth-to-mouth?"

Mariah closed her eyes again, shuddering as she recalled her poor display of gratitude. His face had been familiar, but she couldn't quite put a name to him. "I think I've seen him at school, or around somewhere...." And then she sat up as it hit her. In the kitchen at the Manor, talking to the man in charge of the renovation.

"He's part of the construction staff at school," she said.

Parker's smile waned. "I was hoping he was young and handsome."

Mariah was confused. "He was young. And if you like that rough look, he's handsome."

Now Parker appeared confused. "But I have regular appointments for all the Ripley Construction guys, and the youngest one's in his late forties. Three brothers and two brothers-in-law."

"Guys who work construction," Mariah asked in disbelief, "get massages?"

Parker shifted her weight impatiently. "Well, of course they do. Massage is very sensible. They sling around heavy stuff all day long, reach and bend. It's very forward-thinking of their boss to see that they have weekly appointments.''

"This man was probably in his early to middle thirties," Mariah insisted. "And..." Her attention drifted for a moment as she recalled waking up and looking into his eyes—a soft hazel. "His eyes were hazel.''

"Cam Trent?" Parker said, suddenly animated again. "The plumber? I know he's the plumber on the job because my office is near Whitcomb's Wonders. I've gotten to know all the guys a bit.''

"Whitcomb's what?''

"Wonders. Guys who can do anything." Parker hugged her as if to congratulate her. "He's gorgeous! And smart. He's getting an MBA from Amherst. Wants to be a developer. Addy told me all about him.''

Parker was so enthusiastic that Mariah had to put a stop to her sister's considerations of romance immediately. "Well, he's not going to want anything to do with me. I hit him.''

"You what?" Parker was as horrified as Mariah had hoped.

"I hit him. When I woke up, he was half lying on me, kissing me—or so I thought. By the time I realized he was just...well...I'd already hit him.'' She wasn't being entirely honest, but it was all her sister had to know for now.

The doctor reappeared with a bottle of painkillers on the chance that her headache worsened.

Parker took them from him and introduced herself.

The doctor held up two fingers and asked Mariah how many she saw. When she answered correctly, he asked her name. He listed three items, then asked her to repeat them. She did.

He told Parker to wake her every four hours to test her awareness. "If she seems confused or uncertain, bring her back in."

Parker drove home to her duplex across the street from the grade school. She held Mariah's arm solicitously as they walked from the car to the front door.

"How's the head?" she inquired as she unlocked the door.

"A little woozy," Mariah admitted, "but not awful."

The lock gave, and Parker pushed the door open and reached in to flip on a light. Sheer fabric festooned the living room, leading from a ring in the middle of the ceiling and catching in drapery loops in each corner of the room. Large, colorful pillows lay strewn around the Japanese-restaurant banquette—her sister's creative approach to a "conversation area." A filigreed cage held a fat aromatic candle, which Parker went to light as Mariah eased herself onto the banquette.

"Lavender and chamomile for serenity," Parker said as the wick caught flame. "In fact, if we mixed chamomile with oil of basil, it'd probably be better for you than whatever's in here." She rattled the bottle of painkillers. "But I'll get you water for your pill, and I'm sure you'll feel better before you know it."

Mariah wanted to believe that. Much as she loved her sister's company, she always felt as if she was in purdah with the rest of the harem when she came here, waiting for the sultan to make his nightly choice of woman.

"I know you hate the hammocks." Parker's voice drifted back to the living room as she disappeared into the kitchen. She returned with a glass of water and the bottle of pills. "So we'll sleep down here. You can have the couch and I'll use the beanbag. Want a cookie?"

"No, thanks." Mariah sat up to take her pill, then handed back the water. "There's no reason for you to stay downstairs, Parker. I'll be fine."

"No, you might need me." She put the glass and pills on the low table and sat beside Mariah. "This happens so seldom that I hate to miss it. You're usually the one who rescues me."

Mariah stretched her legs out in front of her and leaned sideways onto Parker's shoulder. "A little financial help now and then hardly constitutes rescue." Mariah had sent her sister money when her first husband had run out on her and left her owing back rent and many overdue bills. Parker's second husband had supported a mistress on the side with money Parker made waiting tables while she went to school to learn massage. He, too, had abandoned her when the mistress's former boyfriend came looking for him.

"You have to make better choices in men, though," Mariah said sleepily. "Stop supporting them and find someone who'll work with you for a change."

Parker put an arm around her and sighed. "I know. It's just that all that sunshine and harmony we got from Mom and Dad really sank in with me. You were more resistant. You're probably a throwback to Grandma Prudie, who loved them both but was convinced they were crazy."

Grandma Prudie had been their father's mother, an Iowa farmwife who related to the earth, all right, but only because it bestowed the fruits of an individual's labor. She thought her son and his wife's belief in the earth's unqualified bounty, in man's intrinsic goodness and life's promised good fortune were poppycock. And she'd said so many times before she died.

Mariah had loved her parents' generous natures and their obvious delight in everything, but she'd never been able to understand such innocence in functioning adults. Until she'd finally grasped that—whether deliberate or simply naive—it brought them aid from everyone. Neighbors admired their sunny dispositions and gave them things—firewood, a side of beef, help with bills—so that they could maintain a lifestyle everyone else knew better than to expect. This had confused Mariah for a long time, until she concluded that it was still proof of man's basic goodness—his willingness to support in a friend what he knew he couldn't have for himself.

"I feel that my life's been very blessed," Parker continued, "and that I have a lot of blessings to return. So I try to help those in need."

Mariah yawned. "Yeah, well, some people are just in want, Parker, not need. It's noble to help, but not to let yourself be used."

"I know. I'm off men for a while. How 'bout you?"

"I'm off them forever."

"That isn't healthy. You want children."

Mariah sat up to frown at her. "Park, have you missed the last year of my life? I'm not going to *have* children."

Parker took advantage of the moment to place a pillow on the banquette and reach into a bamboo shelf for a folded afghan. She pointed Mariah to the pillow and covered her with the crocheted blanket.

"I know you're not going to give birth to them, but there are other ways to get them. Just because Ben wouldn't do it doesn't mean you can't do it on your own."

Mariah was about to shake her head, then decided that would not be a good idea. She simply placed it on the pillow, instead. "I don't want them anymore. It's just all too much trouble. Children should have two parents, and men are just too determined to form a dynasty, you know?"

"Well, Ben was. But that doesn't mean they all are." Parker's voice suddenly changed tone from grave to excited. "And a gorgeous plumber has just breathed life back into you! It could be fate has plans for him to give you more than simply oxygen."

Mariah groaned and leaned deeper into the pillow. "Park," she said, her sleepy voice muffled. "Don't even start."

She drifted off to her sister's reply: "Sometimes, Mariah, fate moves whether we're ready or not."

HANK WHITCOMB HAD ARRIVED to work with the cleanup crew. Cam met him in front of the carriage house while carrying his tools back to his truck. He'd long ago walked Brian to the Lightfoot ladies' residence on the other side of the campus, where they'd taken all the other children when the water cleanup had proved too noisy and disruptive for them to stay. It was 2:00 a.m.

Talking with him was a small, very pregnant dark-haired woman with a camera around her neck and pad and pen in the hand she held up to stifle a yawn. She was Haley Megrath, Hank's sister, and publisher of the *Maple Hill Mirror*.

She and Hank came to his truck as he set his tools down on the drive.

"Hi, Cam," Haley said with another yawn as she walked past him toward the steps. "You'd think people could have their crises during the day, when plumbers and reporters are awake, wouldn't you?''

"Yes, you would. Maybe the *Mirror* could launch a campaign toward that end.''

She waved and kept walking. "I'll see what I can do. 'Night, guys.''

"I'll wait for you and follow you home,'' Hank called after her.

She turned at the top. "I'm fine. Go home to Jackie.''

"I'll buy you a mocha at the Breakfast Barn on the way.''

She grinned. "Okay. Who cares about Jackie.'' She blew him a kiss and disappeared inside.

Hank opened the lid of the truck's toolbox for Cam. "One of our more dramatic messes,'' he said with a laugh. "Hey, Freddy!'' He patted the back window as Fred's head appeared. The dog was barking excitedly. Hank leaned an elbow on the side of the truck as Cam put away his tools. "I hear you rescued Mariah Mercer from drowning.''

Cam shook his head. "That's a little overstated. Brian—one of the kids—held her head out of the water. I just carried her to a bed.''

"Where you gave her mouth-to-mouth and she French-kissed you.''

Cam frowned. "No, she didn't.''

"Yes, she did. Ashley told me.'' Hank grinned. "She's thrilled about it. She adores Mariah and thinks it'd be wonderful if she could find a husband."

Cam gave Hank a shove out of his way as he dropped pipes into the back. "Yeah, well, I don't think Mariah Mercer has designs on me. After she kissed me, she slugged me."

"Really?"

"Yeah. Probably a reaction to the bump on the head, or something. No big deal."

"So I can tell my mother you're still on the market?"

Cam opened the passenger side of the cab to let Fred out, the gesture half practical, half vengeful. The dog leaped on him elatedly, then went right to Hank, who always had treats in his pockets. Fred backed Hank up to the side of the truck, his paws on his chest, alternately kissing him and barking a demand for treats.

Pinned to the truck, Hank reached into a pants pocket. "How big is this guy going to get?" he asked, quickly putting a biscuit in the dog's mouth. "He doesn't beg—he just mugs you for what he wants!"

"I'm not sure. I guess some Labs get to a hundred pounds or more. Jimmy didn't tell me that when he sold him to me." Jimmy Elliott was a fireman and another of Whitcomb's Wonders.

Treat in his mouth, Fred ran off around the side of the carriage house.

"You must be beat," Hank said. "You have a class in the morning?"

"In the afternoon. I'll be fine. I'm a little wired, actually. Letty brought us coffee and I don't think she bothered to grind the beans."

Hank took a key out of his jacket pocket and offered it to Hank. "Why don't you go take a look at the lake house," he suggested. "You and Fred can even sleep there if you don't want to go back home tonight."

Cam tried to push the key away. "Hank, I appreciate the offer to buy your house. There's not a place in town I'd like better. But I keep telling you—I don't have the cash."

Hank nodded. They'd argued this before. "We'll find a way to keep the payments way down."

Hank had married Jackie Fortin, the mayor of Maple Hill, a brief two months ago. In doing so, he'd acquired two little girls, ages seven and eleven, and infant twin boys. He'd bought the big house on the lake as a bachelor, but now found that the old family home Jackie occupied was closer to school for the girls, and closer to city hall for Jackie and for Hank, since the office of Whitcomb's Wonders was located in its basement.

Cam had mentioned once at a party Hank had held how ideal he thought the house was, how warm and welcoming after his cramped apartment behind the fire station.

"We'll put a balloon payment at the end," Hank

said, "and by then you'll be a well-known developer. Since you have plans to save our colonial charm rather than replace it with malls and movieplexes, you'll be popular and make big bucks."

"That's a little optimistic."

"It never hurts to think positive." Hank took his hand and slapped the key into it. "Even though that hasn't been your experience in the past. You have control now. You're not dependent upon neglectful parents, and you don't have to worry about a selfish wife. Do what *you* want to do."

Cam was touched by his concern and grateful for his support. "You're pretty philosophical for a NASA engineer-turned-electrician. You didn't get zapped tonight while standing in all that water, did you?"

"No." Hank grinned and braced his stance as Fred came running back to them. "I'm charged on life, pal...charged on life. Oof! Go look at the house. Fred needs room to run. And someday you'll want to think about getting married again and having children."

Well, he was right about Fred needing room to run, anyway. Cam closed the dog in the car, said good-night to Hank and the cleaning crew still working, waved at Haley, who photographed them, then headed for home. But somewhere along the way he took a turn toward Maple Hill Lake and Hank's house on the less-populated far side of it.

He pulled off the road onto a private drive that

led through a high hedge, and into the driveway of the two-story split-level. He would look through it as Hank suggested, get the notion of buying it out of his system. Then he could just settle down, keep working and going to school so that he could finally achieve the goal for which he'd come here. He wanted an MBA behind him before he bought the old Chandler Mill outside of town and turned it into office space and apartments.

He'd talked to Evan Braga about it, and he thought the idea was sound. Braga was another of Hank's men who did painting and wallpapering, and sold real estate on the side. He'd been a cop in Boston and had come to Maple Hill for the same reason Cam had—to start over. He hadn't said why and Cam hadn't asked.

Anyway…if he was going to buy a house in Maple Hill, it should be one of the classic salt boxes or Georgians that were such a part of the area's history.

But he loved this house. From the moment he'd arrived at Hank's party all those months ago, he'd felt as if the house had a heartbeat.

He let himself in and flipped on the light in the front room. Fred stayed right beside him intimidated by the new surroundings. As Cam walked from room to room, he became aware of details he hadn't noticed before. The master bedroom had a fireplace that was also open to the bathroom, which had two sinks and vanities, a sunken tub and greenery growing all around it. It was probably what a Roman bath would have looked like. He could imagine lying in the tub after a particularly grueling and dirty day in the pipes, and being warmed by a real fire. Here was a tendency toward hedonism he didn't even realize he had. Each of the three bedrooms upstairs had a private bath.

He walked back downstairs to look around outside and Fred went wild, running through the tall grass that rimmed the lake, chasing imaginary quarry in the dark. He stopped to sniff the air and bark his delight to the woods across the road.

The property spread for five acres in both directions, and except for Fred's footsteps, there was nothing but the sound of insects. The natural perfume of the dark quiet night took his breath away.

A broad deck ran all around the house, and Cam remembered Hank saying that when he'd bought the place, he'd anticipated having barbecues and inviting his friends. But Whitcomb's Wonders had been more successful than even he'd imagined, and family life had kept him too busy.

Cam looked at the covered gas grill in a corner of the porch, and the wide picnic table beside it. "I could have the guys over for a barbecue," he thought aloud. He could get a small boat and go fishing.

As a child, he'd never been able to bring anyone home because of the unpredictable condition of his parents. He'd dreamed of inviting friends over, hosting parties, having a Christmas open house the way his friends' parents did.

A curious hopefulness stirred in the middle of his chest. He could do that here. He could...maybe...someday...give some thought to getting married again, having a family.

"Oh, whoa!" he said to himself.

Fred, hearing the command and thinking it applied to him, came racing back. Cam caught him as he jumped against his chest.

"I'm getting carried away here, Fred," he said, going back to the front door to make sure he'd locked it. "That's the trouble with having a cold, grim childhood and a selfish wife. You get a glimpse of warmth and happiness and you become this greedy monster, wanting more and more."

Fred raced around his legs, apparently seeing nothing wrong with that.

Cam tested the doorknob and, finding it secure, led the way back to the truck and the little apartment behind the fire station. So he had cardiac arrest every time the alarm went off. He was learning to live with it.

He didn't need the house. And so far his life had taught him that you didn't always get what you needed, much less what you wanted.

CHAPTER FOUR

THE ALARM SHRIEKED in Cam's ear. Without moving his head from the pillow, he reached out to slam it off.

Blessed quiet.

He'd finally gone to bed at 4:00 a.m. and set the alarm for seven. There was too much to do at the school today to allow for eight hours' sleep. But certainly he could steal another fifteen minutes.

Fred, however, had other plans. The Lab, awake at the foot of the bed and waiting for the smallest sign that Cam was awake, leaped onto his chest and bathed his face with dog kisses.

Cam tried to push him away, but he was weak after the all-night session and the measly three hours' sleep. The dog plopped down on top of him and chewed on his chin.

Cam knew if he didn't get up he'd be eaten. It would be done with affection, but he'd be eaten.

"Okay, Fred, that's enough," he said calmly but firmly, pushing the dog off.

He sat up to swing his legs over the side of the bed just as Fred decided he'd cooperated long enough and it was time for some serious extreme wrestling. Growling, large mouth open in what Cam thought of as his alligator mode, Fred attacked.

Cam's body, unfortunately aimed toward the edge of the bed, went over the side, dog atop him and gleefully pretending to kill him.

MARIAH HEADED FROM THE CAR where Parker waited, along the little walkway to the stairs that led up to Cameron Trent's apartment. She'd awakened this morning determined to apologize to the man who'd given her mouth-to-mouth resuscitation and been slapped for his efforts.

Provided the man was Cameron Trent. And provided he would even want to listen to her. She intended to reassure him quickly that she would take only a moment of his time, then she would never darken his doorway again.

She climbed the stairs, rehearsing her little speech. "Mr. Trent, I apologize for slapping you. I thought you were my…" No. That was too much information.

"Mr. Trent, I apologize for slapping you. I was in a sort of dream state and your lips were…" No, no! Too revealing of feelings she didn't understand and he was bound to misinterpret.

"Mr. Trent, I'm sorry I hit you. I awoke to see a stranger leaning over me and I…I…"

Okay, get it straight! She told herself firmly. *Don't stammer like an idiot.* Maybe a simple "I'm sorry.'' He'd know what she was sorry about, so there was little point in belaboring why it had happened.

She checked the note in her hand. Apartment E. Parker had called Addy at the Breakfast Barn, where she always had breakfast with her cronies, and learned Trent's address.

She stopped in front of the end apartment upstairs, pulled aside the screen door and, bracing herself, knocked lightly twice. The door squeaked open.

She heard a commotion beyond the door and concluded he must have the television on. She knocked a little louder. The door opened farther, making the commotion inside more audible.

But it wasn't the television. Someone was being attacked! By...dogs? In Maple Hill? The man's cries sounded desperate. She looked around for help, but Parker couldn't see her from the car.

She couldn't just walk away. This man had possibly saved her life; the least she could do was make an effort for him.

She looked around for a weapon and, finding none, simply took a firm hold of the handle of her purse, burst through the door and ran toward the sound.

In a bedroom at the back of the house, she found a sight that chilled her. The man whose face she'd awakened to yesterday now lay half on and half off the bed, his legs trapped in the blankets while a huge black beast, fangs bared, attacked him unmercifully, sounding like one of the dogs of hell unleashed.

She fought a trembling in her limbs and advanced, swinging at the glossy hindquarters with her purse. "Stop it!" she shrieked at the animal. "Get out! Get out!" The dog yelped and withdrew onto the bed, eyes wide. Encouraged that she'd made it retreat, she followed it, purse in full swing.

"Whoa!" the man shouted.

His directive didn't register, however, as she climbed onto the bed in pursuit of her quarry. "Get out of here you—"

Her threat was abruptly silenced as something strong manacled her ankle, effectively dropping her facedown into the bedclothes.

Momentarily blinded and unable to move, she felt a cold chill as she heard a menacing growl just above her.

"Fred!" Trent shouted. "Down! Now!"

She heard the dog's claws connect with the hard-wood floor.

Fred? Cameron Trent had been viciously attacked by a dog named…Fred?

CAM WAS SURE HE WAS hallucinating. First of all, there was a woman in his bedroom, and that hadn't happened in a long time. Second, she appeared to be an avenging angel determined to rescue him from Fred's morning wake-up ritual. An angel he'd rescued himself just last night. Only, she hadn't reacted like much of an angel.

It took a moment before he realized her determination to save him included hitting his dog with a leather purse that resembled something Evander Holyfield would hang from the ceiling and beat with boxing gloves. And then he reached up and caught her foot.

She plopped down in the middle of his mattress, skirt halfway up her legs, one shoe off, the other dangling from her toe. He experienced a sudden visceral need to put his hand to the back of her thigh and explore upward.

Fortunately—or unfortunately—his foster parents' civilizing influence had taken root in him and he simply freed her ankle and got to his feet. Then, remembering he was wearing only white cotton briefs, he wrapped an old brown blanket around his waist as she rolled over.

She wasn't happy.

He wasn't surprised.

For an instant he simply absorbed the steamy look of her in his bed. She wore another long-sleeved silky blouse, pale blue this time, and another long skirt—black. Her hair was in a tight knot at the back of her head; her cheeks were flushed from exertion.

Nothing about her should have been seductive, but there she was amid his rumpled bedclothes, knees bared, one tendril of dark hair falling from her right temple. Her eyes smoldered.

He concluded that expression was probably fueled by anger or embarrassment, but what it contributed to the picture she made was powerful. He wanted her. Badly.

But what was she doing here?

Fred, standing near the edge of the bed, leaned a long neck and tongue forward and slurped her bare knee.

She shrank back with a little cry.

"Fred!" Cam caught the dog's collar and made him sit. Fred complied, apparently totally affronted.

"I'm sorry," Cam said quickly as Mariah looked around herself, her cheeks growing rosy. So it was embarrassment. "I know that appeared brutal, but it's a game we play. Fred's just seven months old and very frisky. The snarling and teeth flashing are phony. He's just trying to get me up for breakfast."

She drew a deep breath and something inside her seemed to collapse. He wasn't sure what that meant, but he didn't like the look of it. Her eyes lost their smolder and filled with the sadness he'd seen in them last night.

Instinctively, he reached for her waist to pluck her off the bed and stand her on the floor. In her stocking feet, she barely skimmed his shoulder. "I appreciate the rescue, though," he said, his hands still on her. "I'll bet that purse packs a wallop."

She put her hands on his and removed them from her waist. "Where *is* my purse?" she asked stiffly.

It had gone over the side of the bed when she'd

fallen. He went to retrieve it for her. It weighed a ton.

When he came back with it, she was hunting for her second shoe. Then she looked beyond him and gasped. Fred, whom he'd lost track of when he'd scooped her off the bed, had it in his teeth.

"Fred, give me that shoe!" she demanded, going toward the dog with a hand outstretched.

"Mariah…" Cam began to caution, but he was too late. The dog had darted off toward the living room, tail wagging, and Mariah went in pursuit.

Cam followed, catching up with them in the kitchen. Mariah had one end of the shoe and Fred the other. This could not end well.

"Mariah, don't pull!" he ordered. Then to the dog, he said in the authoritative tone he'd learned in obedience class, "Fred, give!"

It never worked in class, either. Fred was an independent thinker.

Cam finally grabbed the dog around the jaw and pried the shoe from his teeth. There was a small tooth hole in the side of the black leather flat, and slobber on the toe. He wiped it off with the tail of the blanket wrapped around him and handed the shoe to her.

She snatched it from him and slipped it on, the smolder back in her eyes. "Thank you!" she snapped. "I came here in an attempt to be a thoughtful human being, and thanks to you and Mr. Astaire here—" she pointed in the direction of the dog

"—or is it Flintstone? Regardless, I've been harassed and embarrassed!"

"I'm sorry you were embarrassed," he said reasonably, "but I didn't expect visitors this morning."

"Then you should have locked your door." She marched back to the bedroom, where she'd left her purse. "I thought you were being killed!"

He tried to placate her with "You were very heroic."

"No, I was mistaken." She made that correction grimly as she shouldered her purse.

"Is that such a terrible thing?" he asked quietly. "Or is it just that making mistakes is new to you?"

She blew air scornfully. "I've made a lot of mistakes. But I'm trying to change the pattern."

Fred had followed them back to the bedroom and she leaned down to stroke the dog's head. He reacted with his customary enthusiasm and was about to lick her face.

Cam caught him before he could connect, but Mariah surprised him by leaning down to take one of Fred's kisses, then laughing as she nuzzled his face with her own.

"It's okay, Fred," she said. "I know you didn't mean any harm. I'm sorry I yelled at you."

Cam, now completely confused about her—and just as captivated—asked innocently, "Aren't you sorry you yelled at me?"

HE *WAS* GORGEOUS NOW THAT she observed him with all her faculties at work. She hadn't appreciated the width of his shoulders last night, the odd gold color of his eyes. His good looks weren't a feature-by-feature thing but rather a whole impression made by confidence and humor playing in the rough angles.

She frowned and folded her arms. "Did I yell at you?"

He pretended hurt feelings in a theatrically dramatic sniff. "Yes, you yelled at me. You blamed me for what you called your 'embarrassment,' and here I was the one wearing nothing but my skivvies when you burst in. And in danger of being puppy chow, if you'll recall."

She wanted to laugh. Nothing made her laugh these days—except children and dogs. "You assured me you were in no danger."

He folded his arms over that formidable chest and looked away in a gesture of emotional delicacy. "Because I didn't want you to risk yourself further on my behalf."

She still managed to keep a straight face. "Well, I appreciate that. I have to go."

She headed for the door again, but he caught her halfway across the living room and turned her around. His hand was warm and strong and stopped her cold though he applied no pressure.

"What was the thoughtful reason you came?" he asked. There was something urgent in his eyes.

"Oh." She sighed, realizing she'd never offered her apology. "I forgot." She angled her chin, hop-

ing to put him off by appearing haughty. Men usually hated that. And she did not want to be attracted
to this one. "I came to apologize for slapping you
last night. I was…" What was it she had rehearsed?
He was gazing into her eyes and she couldn't remember. "I was sort of dreaming and you…and
I…" She stopped, hating that she was stammering
like a twit. She squared her shoulders and tried to
go on. "When I woke up, I thought you were…"
She did everything humanly possible to avoid com-
pleting that sentence, avoid uttering the word that
dangled unspoken.

"You thought I was kissing you?" he prompted,
apparently having no such compunction.

He didn't really appear self-satisfied, but there
was an artlessness to him she didn't trust at all.

"Yes," she admitted, making herself look into his
eyes. "I'm sorry."

She tried to leave again, but he still had her arm.
She felt a sudden and desperate need to get out of
there.

"What?" she demanded impatiently.

"I haven't accepted your apology," he reminded
her.

She cocked an eyebrow at him. "What?"

"Well, how I react to this," he explained in an
amiable tone, "will be determined by why you hit
me."

"I just told you! I was dreaming and I…"

"I know, but if you were angry at me because

you were disappointed that I *wasn't* kissing you, that requires a different response altogether.''

She knew where this was going and she didn't want any part of it. Well, she did, but only for purely selfish reasons. She missed the intimacy of marriage. Not the sex, necessarily, but the touches, the pats, the…the kisses. And though she'd sworn there would never be another man in her life, she was still allowed to miss what a man brought to a relationship. Wasn't she?

''I thought you were…'' She even hated to say his name aloud. It brought back memories of those last awful few months of her marriage when she'd shouted it pleadingly, begging Ben to understand how she felt.

Cam waited.

''My…husband,'' she said finally.

His eyes closed a moment. ''You have a husband?''

That was her out. She had simply to say yes, and he'd lose interest in this unsettling morning exercise. Freedom was one small word away.

She opened her mouth to speak it but heard herself say, instead, ''My ex-husband.''

He looked cautious. ''You want him back?'' he asked gently.

For the first time in a year she faced that question directly. Did she want him back?

''No,'' she whispered. ''But I miss…'' It was hard to say.

"You can tell me," he encouraged her softly.

The words clogged her throat. What had begun in amusement and sexual challenge was all of a sudden filled with real emotion.

"I miss trust," she finally admitted, her voice barely audible, even to herself. He tipped her face up as if to help himself hear. "I miss holding hands, telling stories, and I miss..." She had to say it. "Kisses."

And that seemed to be all he had to know. This was no longer about what she'd felt last night when she slapped him, but what was suddenly between them now as she admitted need and he responded.

His mouth came down on hers with tender authority. The sureness in the hands that framed her face told her to leave it to him; he knew what he was doing. And he did.

The touch of his lips was familiar from last night, and she experienced none of the awkward newness of first kisses. He was confident, she was willing, and the chemistry was its own catalyst.

His mouth was dry and warm and clever, his hands sure as they moved over her back, down her spine, stopping at the hollow just below her waist, then moving up again.

She met his lips avidly, basking in the almost-forgotten comfort of the shelter of a man's arms.

HER RESPONSE WAS FAR MORE enthusiastic than Cam had expected. He wasn't entirely sure what was happening here, except that it wasn't what he'd originally intended. He'd been teasing her, playing with their previous connection, trying to taunt the stiffness out of her because...he wasn't sure why. Stiff, tight women weren't his type. And neither were small ones. They made him feel huge and inept and afraid to move.

But she wrapped her arms around him gamely, dipped the tip of her tongue into his mouth with tantalizing eagerness, combed her fingers into the hair at the back of his neck and somehow touched something inside him that seemed to rip in two everything he thought he'd decided about women since his first wife, Allison.

Then without warning she sagged against him, dropping her forehead to his chest and remaining absolutely still for several seconds. When she raised her head, her eyes were stormy with something he couldn't quite define.

She punched his shoulder as if to release some pent-up emotion. But it didn't seem to be anger.

"Now you're going to have to come back tomorrow," he said, trying to lighten the abrupt sadness in the room, "and apologize for hitting me again."

"So this is what's taking so long," a female voice said from the doorway.

Cam looked up and Mariah started guiltily out of his arms.

"Parker!" she said, her voice sounding strangled.

"I'm sorry I kept you waiting. I thought the dog was devouring him and came in to…"

Parker glanced at Cam, still partially wrapped in a blanket, then listened interestedly as Mariah tried to explain, then gave up. It did sound ridiculous.

"Oh, never mind." Mariah looked up at Cam, opened her mouth to speak, then apparently decided against it. "Goodbye," she said, instead. She walked past Parker and out the door. Fred whined.

"Good morning, Parker," Cam said politely, feigning a normalcy the situation denied.

Parker, who'd always been warm and kind to him the few times they'd met in city hall, now studied him with a measure of doubt. "Mariah's my sister," she said.

He nodded. "Hank told me." He explained briefly about Fred and his growling game. "It was 4:00 a.m. when I got home. I pulled my shoes and socks off on the porch because I was drenched, came in with an armload of stuff and kicked the door closed—or thought I had. When Mariah heard Fred playing, she assumed I was in trouble and came in to rescue me."

"That kiss was a thank-you?" she queried.

"No," he replied. "You should probably ask her what it was."

She nodded and prepared to leave. He walked her to the door, where she stopped and smiled. "She's a very nice girl who's had a very bad time recently."

He leaned a shoulder in the doorway. "The ex-husband?"

Parker looked surprised. "She told you?"

"Only that she had one."

"He was a good guy," Parker explained, "who turned out to be a bastard. I'd hate to have that happen to her again."

"Don't worry, she's learned to defend herself," he said with a wry smile. "She keeps hitting me."

Parker frowned. "She came to apologize for that."

He laughed lightly. "She did. Then she hit me again." He straightened and assured her seriously, "I'm not a bastard. My background isn't pretty and I wouldn't claim to be a good guy, but I'm not a threat to anybody's safety, either."

She studied him, as if deciding whether or not to believe him. Then she finally nodded. "Okay. I'll take your word on that. Otherwise, I know how to massage your shoulder into your eye socket."

"Rough women in your family," he noted with a grin.

She smiled pleasantly and hurried down the stairs.

Cam closed and locked the door, fed Fred, then decided against cereal in favor of stopping at Perk Avenue coffee shop on his way to work. He deserved a little sugar after what he'd been through this morning.

In the bedroom, he yanked off the blanket, delved into the closet for fresh jeans and a sweatshirt and started toward the bathroom, but something sparkling in the middle of the bed caught his attention. He reached for it and found that it was a little gold hoop with three tiny beads—an earring. Mariah's earring.

He tossed it in his hand, remembering her leaping to his rescue, sprawled in the middle of his bed, leaning into him as he kissed her.

He had to draw a breath to clear the images. He didn't need this. If he did intend to get involved with a woman, he wanted some buxom, uncomplicated ray of sunshine who'd want to make a home, raise children and help him forget all he'd lost or never had.

He didn't need a tiny brunette with troubled eyes who'd had ''a hard time.''

He tossed the earring again as he headed for the bathroom, caught it, then stopped with a growl of complaint when it bit into his hand. He opened his palm to find that his overzealous grab had caused the sharp post to jab his ring finger.

A metaphor for his involvement with her? he wondered.

CHAPTER FIVE

THE SECOND MORNING AFTER the deluge, Mariah encouraged her little troupe to finish breakfast so that they could get to school on time. They were rushed this morning. Mariah had overslept—something she never did—and it had taken Ashley's violent shaking to wake her up.

"I'm sorry I have to hurry you," she explained, shooing the girls upstairs to brush their teeth. "I know it's all my fault, but we can still be on time if we put some effort into it.

"We were late yesterday," Philip said, "and nobody cared."

"That was because of the excitement the night before. But today it's our responsibility to be punctual."

"There's still no carpet," Amy complained as she and the other girls started up the stairs.

Mariah nodded. "We have to wait for the wood to dry. It'll be replaced at the end of the week."

"So, where do you think the gold is?" Peter asked Brian as the three boys, teeth already brushed, shouldered their backpacks.

Brian considered. "Cam says I have to do more research."

"Well, where else could it be?" Philip asked.

"I'm thinking maybe in…"

Mariah missed whatever it was he thought as he lowered his voice to a whisper.

Brian had dropped Cam's name at every opportunity since the flood. The boy had acquired status among the other children because the man who'd rescued Mariah had asked him to help. He was clearly enjoying his popularity.

Mariah tried not to think about that night—or yesterday morning. Her behavior in Cam's apartment had to have been a result of her embarrassment at discovering that he hadn't been in danger at all, simply playing with Fred. Added to that was the fact that she hadn't seen a partially naked man in a long time, and the fact that the hormones she'd been sure had died with her marriage were still very lively. She had to have lost her mind just a bit.

Otherwise, why would she have practically asked him to kiss her?

Why would she have enjoyed it?

Why could she still feel his lips on hers twenty-five hours later?

It didn't matter, she told herself briskly, pushing chairs up to the kitchen table. Unless there was another plumbing emergency, she wouldn't have to see him again. And if there was, she could ask one of the Lightfoot sisters to attend to it. They were full of praise for his work—and his charm.

Even Parker had nice things to say about him, though she'd found them in each other's arms.

"He seems to be a gentleman," she'd insisted, when Mariah had grumbled in response to her question about what had been going on when she'd walked in on them.

Mariah hadn't denied it, but wondered why, if he was such a gentleman, he made her feel such unladylike things.

The girls bustled down the stairs, dragging backpacks.

Mariah rounded up her little group and led them outside, locking the carriage house door behind her. They went down through a lane of swamp maple to the school playground, where all the day children were gathered, waiting for classes to begin. A lively basketball game was under way, several girls were jumping rope and a coed group competed for daredevil notoriety on the monkey bars.

Janie Florio, a third-grade teacher, waved at Mariah from the basketball hoop, fulfilling her role as playground monitor.

Mariah returned the wave and was about to wish the children a good day, when she realized they'd already dispersed into their playgroups without giving her a second thought.

Little ingrates, she thought good-naturedly as she

climbed the stairs to attend a meeting with Letitia Lightfoot.

Letty hadn't specified the reason for the meeting, but Mariah could only assume it had to do with the flood. A lot of damage had been done in the carriage house, though mercifully it was mostly superficial and covered by insurance. She would probably suggest Mariah be more vigilant, more of an authority figure with the children than the friend she strove to be.

Letitia's office was clearly not dedicated to the needs of the children. Everywhere else in the building the rooms were cheerfully academic—blackboards, maps all over, alphabets and musical notes running above the picture rails. Here, there were big cozy chairs, frilly lamps, a mantel covered with family photos, lace curtains at the window.

The other Lightfoot sister sat behind a smallish rosewood desk and pointed Mariah to a chair patterned in cabbage roses.

Mariah sat, sinking into the old springs. Letty, she thought, looked severe. She couldn't have heard about the kiss, could she? Of course not. The only other person who knew, aside from herself and Cam, was Parker, and she wouldn't have told.

Such behavior had been irresponsible, very inappropriate in a woman hired to guard the safety of young…

"Mariah," Letitia said without preamble, "we've finally decided to close the dormitory at the end of this school year.'' She sighed after she spoke, as if making herself say the words had taken a lot of energy. "I'll be contacting the parents and Ashley's guardian today to let them know. I'd like you to tell the children.''

Mariah wasn't shocked; the rumor had circulated for some time. But she was upset at the realization that she'd lose her charges, not just for the summer but forever.

And what about Ashley, whose guardian was ill, and Brian, whose mother was in and out of rehab? What would they do without the stabilizing influence of the Maple Hill Manor School? Public schools were wonderful, of course, but the Manor's program was set up to take special care of children in their unique situations.

"I don't want you to worry about your position here,'' Letty continued. "We've all grown very fond of you. It's clear you're destined to work with children and we'll find another spot for you by September. Lavinia thinks we need an office secretary, but I think your special talents would be wasted behind a desk. We'll come up with something suitable, if you'd like to stay on as much as we'd like you to.''

Mariah smiled gratefully. "I so appreciate that, Letty. But, you know that I've been planning an extended European trip. Maybe this is the time for me to go.''

Letty frowned with maternal displeasure. "Well, I'd hoped you'd gotten over that notion. When you hired on, you told me it would be just for a year, that you had this trip planned to tour Europe and learn about art, but I'd put it down to the dreams of a woman who'd lost so much and wanted to escape. I thought you might feel loved and wanted here and decide that escape wasn't the answer.''

''I don't want to escape, Letty,'' Mariah denied gently. ''I just know now that marriage and family aren't for me, so I may as well get out there and find out what it is I do want—and try to learn something in the process.''

Letitia leaned her elbows on the desk and smiled benevolently at Mariah. ''Marriage with *that* man wasn't for you, and neither is having babies in the traditional way. But there's so much more to marriage and family than what you've known.''

Mariah shook her head firmly. ''I don't want that anymore, Letty. I have other plans. And while I appreciate your concern and affection for me, I have to do what I have to do.''

''So you *are* bent on escape.''

''It's not escape. It's exploration.''

Letitia stared at her a moment, then smiled. ''Well. When you return from your exploration, we'll find a place for you if you'd like to work with us again. But until then, we have a lot to do here until the school year's over. Is your heart still in it?''

''Absolutely,'' Mariah replied firmly.

''Good. Then please explain to the children, and we'll try to spoil them to help cheer them up.''

Mariah nodded. "I'm worried about Ashley. Do you have any idea what Walter Kerwin's intentions are for her if he should…"

Letitia shook her head. "That isn't really our business, Mariah. But I'll be speaking with him today, and if he shares any information about that, I'll let you know."

"Thank you, Letty."

"Are you going shopping today?"

Mariah nodded. Every Tuesday morning she replenished the dorm's groceries and picked up special requests for the children.

Letitia delved into a bottom drawer of her desk and surfaced waving a ten-dollar bill. Mariah stood to take it from her. "Would you buy me a quarter pound of raisin clusters? Dark chocolate."

Chocolate was Letitia's one indulgence. Mariah had trouble finding fault with that.

"Of course." Mariah started for the door.

"And about the flood…"

Mariah stopped in her tracks, prepared to take the heat for Brian's gold-digging fiasco. She turned, shoulders square, "Yes?"

Letitia shook her head. "We had Brian's grandfather here in the old days and he set the lawn on fire with a magnifying glass. Unfortunately, we'd just mowed, and it caught a bank of raked grass and burned several acres. We had his mother, too, and she had the same problems when she was in high school that she has now. We had to expel her."

"Mercy."

"Yes. I know there's nothing you could have done to prevent what happened, but it was costly, and we must try to make Brian understand that even if he finds the gold, he'll owe it all to us should he destroy the house."

Relieved, Mariah nodded. "I've already explained that."

"Good. Then enjoy your day."

Mariah left Letitia's office and headed for the cafeteria, hoping to get a quick cup of coffee before she went into town. Because she'd been rushed this morning, she hadn't put up her hair or taken care with her clothes and she felt sort of unguarded, and therefore unprepared. She felt sure caffeine would help.

The cafeteria was filled with workmen, a circumstance the Manor staff had grown used to and mostly ignored. As she stepped over lumber in the dining area, she could hear saws whine, the staccato beat of hammering and the sound of male laughter. She went behind a long counter where lunch was usually served and into the kitchen.

Though the Manor had made arrangements for the public school to cater lunch at tables now set up in the gym until the renovation was complete, a coffeepot was always going in the kitchen for the staff and the workmen.

She took a thick pottery cup from a tray on the stainless-steel counter and filled it with the steaming brew. She turned to find a quiet corner in which to drink it—and ran right into Cam Trent, who was coming up behind her.

She uttered a little cry of dismay as the coffee sloshed; he danced back a step, and she put a hand to her cup as if to hold the coffee in. The hot brew sloshed all over it and she cried out again.

"Mariah!" Cam took the cup from her, caught her wrist and led her to the sink, where he slapped on the cold water tap and dunked her hand under it. "I'm sorry. I thought you saw me."

"I had my back to you," she pointed out, though her brain seemed focused on the touch of his fingertips at her wrist. "How could I have seen you?"

He turned her hand over under the water, his glance at her friendly but unsettlingly sharp. "I sensed you before I saw you," he said. "I thought it might have been the same for you."

She ignored that, determined just to get out of there. Her pulse was fluttering.

He shut off the water, dried her hand with the tail of his shirt, then inspected it. The pad of her thumb was red where the hot coffee had burned her.

"Come on. I can take care of that." Still holding her hand, he drew her with him out the kitchen's back door.

She pulled against him. "But my coffee..."

He wasn't listening. In another moment they were in a parking area filled with tradesmen's trucks. He led her to a green pickup that had seen better days.

He opened the passenger-side door and was immediately assailed by Fred, who kissed Cam's face and whopped him with a dexterous paw.

"Hey, Fred." Cam patted the dog's flank, then reached around him and into the glove compartment. He extracted a first aid kit.

Fred licked Cam's ear while Cam delved inside. He finally held up a small tube of something. "Hydrocortisone cream," he said as he placed the kit on the roof of the cab. Holding her injured hand palm up, he squirted a small amount of white cream into it.

He rubbed it in gently.

She tried to think of something else. She'd felt flustered and befuddled this morning, and had put it down to oversleeping and then hurrying to prepare for school. His gentle, circling touch didn't help. That is, it soothed the burn but did nothing for her flustered feelings.

"Better?" he asked.

"Yes, thank you," she replied. She looked at her thumb and not at him. Then she focused on the dog, who was overwhelmed by her attention. He kissed her cheek, her forehead, her hair.

"Fred, show some manners!" Cam commanded, pushing him back onto the seat he was about to fall off of.

"That's all right." Mariah patted the dog and nuzzled him. "My husband got our retriever in the divorce and I miss her a lot."

CAM, STANDING SLIGHTLY behind Mariah, put the tube back into the first aid kit, studying her, thinking there was something different about her this morning. She seemed a little less controlled. Then he realized that her hair wasn't scraped back and tied in a knot. It fell to the middle of her back, thick and glossy and the color of walnut. It softened the line of her face, darkened her eyes to midnight. Light rippled in it as she nuzzled Fred. Her hair made Cam feel lustful. He hated being such a cliché, but he couldn't deny his reaction.

"Have you had breakfast?" he asked.

She stepped aside, giving him more room than he needed.

"No, I overslept. But I don't really have time. I have to go shopping and then there's—" A wild rumbling in her stomach interrupted her.

"Sounds like you'd better make time," he said, pushing Fred to the middle of the bench seat. "Besides, I have something of yours."

She looked puzzled. "What?"

"I'll tell you over breakfast," he said, bargaining, "then I'll take you wherever you want to go shopping. I have to pick up a few things, too."

She eyed him doubtfully. "Aren't you supposed to be working?"

"I came in to see if they were ready for me, but they're ironing out some kind of problem with the plan, and I can't start until tomorrow. Climb in." He held the door, waiting for her to comply.

She finally did, giving him a brief but stimulating glimpse of a jeans-clad derriere as she swung into the seat. He pretended detachment, locked her in and closed the door.

He was not only a cliché, he decided as he walked around to his side, but a pubescent cliché.

The Breakfast Barn was everyone's favorite place to begin the day. When things were starting slowly everywhere else, it was alive with activity—businessmen and -women, morning walkers, gossip groups who'd been getting together for years and solved their own and the world's problems over scrambled eggs and coffee.

The Barn was a huge room lined with booths and filled with tables in the middle. The walls were covered with photos of the city teams the restaurant had sponsored, of parties held there, of patrons celebrating one success or another. It was home away from home for much of the population of Maple Hill.

Cam spotted an empty booth near a window and pointed Mariah to it. He followed her across the room, weaving in and out of tables, noting the speculating glances of friends and neighbors.

Rita Robidoux, a fixture at the Barn, was upon them immediately with menus and glasses of water. "Coffee?" she asked.

"Please," Mariah said.

"Regular?"

"Yes, please."

"Coming right up." As she turned away from

Mariah, she waggled her eyebrows at Cam, a silent comment on the worthiness of his breakfast companion.

He gave her a teasing frown of disapproval. "Do you know Mariah Mercer?" he asked politely for Mariah's benefit.

Mariah smiled. "No, we've never—" she began, but Rita was already filling her in on herself.

"You're the dorm mother at the Manor," she said, offering her hand. "Came here from Chicago after a divorce, to be near your sister, Parker Peterson. You never get out to breakfast because you're always overseeing the children's breakfast, but you show up occasionally at dinner with Parker when the Lightfoot ladies give you a day off."

Mariah blinked in astonishment as she shook Rita's hand.

"The rumor," Cam said gravely, "is that Rita has radar and a surveillance truck that she uses to stake out single men to see if they're husband material for the single women on Addy Whitcomb's list. They're a team."

Rita smiled sweetly. "The details are a little off, but essentially, that's correct. I'll be right back with your drinks."

Mariah laughed as Rita wandered off. "So how many women have she and Addy tried to marry you off to?"

"So far I've resisted," he replied. "It helps, too,

that Addy's son is my boss. If she tries to crowd me into a date, Hank finds a plumbing problem for me.''

''You don't want to get married again?''

''I used to think I didn't.''

She'd been perusing the menu but raised her eyes questioningly. ''What changed your mind?''

He knew the menu by heart and pushed his aside. ''Maple Hill, I think. The folks all seem happy, love their spouses, their children, their community. I used to want that in the beginning.''

Now she put her menu aside and focused her attention on him. ''The beginning? Of your life or of your first marriage?''

He leaned back as Rita returned with two cups and a little bowl of creamers, and poured their coffees. She put the pot down on the table, took their orders, then was gone again with another discreet waggle of her eyebrows at Cam.

He put sugar and cream in his coffee, wondering just how much to explain. It was all so grim, and he preferred to think ahead.

''Both, I guess,'' he replied, choosing to skim the surface of the issue. ''I come from a family dedicated to substance abuse and making one another miserable, so as a kid I just didn't believe the cozy families I saw on television. A few of my friends seemed to have them, but I was sure when all their guests were gone, they were just like my family— loud and angry.''

He offered her the cream. She shook her head.

"Allison, my wife," he said, "chose politics over me."

She looked up from placing her napkin over her knee. "You mean, you didn't want her to go into politics? Or she found someone else in politics?"

"First one, then the other," he replied. "My parents have both done time," he said, needing to get past that fact. "My mother's still in prison. Allison was a judge's daughter I'd met at a party. I told her about my family. She said it made no difference to our relationship. I think she even meant it, until someone noticed what a brilliant lawyer she was and asked her to run for local office. I supported that, but someone found out about my family history and decided we should lie about it."

Mariah looked skeptical. "That wouldn't be good, would it? I mean, considering how determined politicians are to unearth what they can use against one another."

He nodded. "That's what I thought. And though I don't like to remember my childhood, I'm proud we survived it. And it's not as if I can erase it."

"So she thought she'd have a better chance without you," she guessed.

"Precisely. She's now married to her campaign manager."

"Who's 'we'?"

For a moment, he wasn't following her.

"You said you were proud 'we' survived it."

"Oh. I have a younger brother and sister. Josh is

a chef in a restaurant in California and has a family. Our little sister, Barbara, took off for New York to be a model. She used to write at first, then she stopped. The last thing we heard was that she had an interview with the Ford agency. She was excited. I can only guess it didn't work out.''

"Have you tried to find her?"

This part was still difficult after all this time. "When her phone didn't answer and she didn't return our calls, I contacted the Ford agency. I was right. They'd decided not to represent her. They had no forwarding address for her. We even hired a private detective and he couldn't find her.''

She said nothing, just waited for more.

"A year later, a call came from a police officer in New York, telling us that Barbara had died from massive injuries sustained in a motorcycle accident. She was twenty-two.''

"Cam, I'm sorry," Mariah said fervently.

He nodded. "The worst part for Josh and me was that for whatever reason, she didn't feel she could call us. I imagine she felt rejected and just didn't think she could come home, even though we sent her to New York with a return ticket.''

She reached across the table to put a hand over his. "Now, there's no way you can blame yourself for that. You can understand her pride being stronger than her need for family, but you can't feel guilty about it. Maybe…maybe she figured after dealing with your parents, you'd seen enough of people who couldn't achieve. She was wrong, of course, but people in pain don't think very clearly.''

He sat in quiet surprise. He'd always looked for the blame in himself. Although their parents had been horrid, he and Josh and Barbara had always stuck together. He'd thought he must have failed in some way to make her understand that whatever happened, she would always be a part of their triumvirate and could seek shelter there anytime. He'd never considered that she might have stayed away to spare him and Josh yet another family failure.

He digested that possibility and felt it soothe him. He finally smiled at Mariah. ''That's an openhearted thought,'' he said.

She inclined her head—the closest she could come to taking a bow in the confining booth. ''My family was good at understanding the souls of people and things, if not at dealing with them very realistically.

''My parents were sort of retread hippies. We lived in communes, in trailers, with friends. The best period of our lives was when we farmed for a cousin of my mother's who'd bought a place as a tax shelter but didn't want to live there. My parents were in heaven and Parker loved it, too.''

He was happy to listen to her talk. She smiled absently and the usually rigid line of her shoulders seemed to relax.

''But I'm a city girl at heart,'' she continued, sitting back in the booth, her hands in her lap. ''My dream is to visit all the great European capitals, learn about Western European art and work on my own.''

''You planning a trip?''

She nodded. ''In my situation at the school, it's been easy to save. And while my ex-husband wasn't willing to share the dog, I did get half our savings account and the proceeds from the sale of our home. I'll be going this summer, I think.''

He felt the smallest pang. Somehow, Mariah leaving felt like…like a missed opportunity. As if he were standing on the brink of something important as it was backing out of reach.

''Money goes pretty quickly when you're spending it and not making more,'' he felt obliged to caution.

She leaned toward him, lowering her voice. ''No!'' she said, pretending surprise. ''I thought it just multiplied in your purse, like an amoeba or whatever it is that splits in two.''

Okay, he had that coming. He stared her down when laughter replaced the seriousness in her eyes, and leaned toward her. ''Well, never having carried a purse, I didn't think that. I thought the bills fooled around in your bank account and generated…interest.''

She laughed. ''Actually,'' she said, ''I paint signs and wall plaques. Gift shops in San Francisco and Chicago carry them for me and I have a dealer in Boston and a separate account to keep track of sales to make sure I am making a profit, and I'm doing well. In fact, I reserved space at St. Anthony's Spring Fair the week after next.''

"Right." He knew about the fair. "Evan Braga belongs to the parish, and I promised to help the men's club with their booth. It's food, I think."

"Who's Evan Braga?"

"He works for Hank, too. He's a house painter, and in his spare time, he sells real estate. We're going to collaborate someday when I buy that old Chandler Mill site and give it a face-lift.''

"When is that going to happen?" she asked, reaching for her coffee cup.

"I'm working on a master's in business administration. I'd like to know more before I start speculating with large amounts of money. Although Evan thinks we should do it now." He grinned. "When the time comes, you'll be welcome to invest your sign fund in my project."

She shook her head. "I should be long gone by then, drifting on a gondola and sketching the Doges' Palace."

The little pang he'd felt the last time she said that doubled in size.

"I hope you find what you're looking for," he said.

To his surprise, she straightened, appearing just a little defensive. "I'm not *looking* for anything," she said. "I just want to see Europe. Why is that so bad?

Parker makes that same criticism. I'm not running away. I'm just…just…''

While she sputtered in an attempt to explain herself, he reached across the table to put a hand over hers. "Hey," he said quietly. "I meant that I hope you'll be happy. That's all. I wasn't implying anything, or suggesting…"

She was still for a moment, her eyes locking with his, their dark depths curiously troubled, her lighthearted mood gone. Then she withdrew her hand.

"I don't see why a woman can't go to Europe," she said, lowering her voice as Rita approached with steaming plates, "without everyone presuming it's an act of cowardice."

There was a commotion as Rita placed a veggie omelet with whole-wheat toast in front of Mariah, and sausage and eggs with biscuits at Cam's place. She pulled ketchup and Tabasco sauce out of her apron pocket, surveyed the table, left and returned instantly to top up their coffees.

"All set?" she asked cheerfully.

Mariah liberally poured Tabasco on her omelet. "Yes, thank you."

Rita observed that and raised an eyebrow at Cam.

"Thanks, Rita," he said quickly, hoping to forestall a comment.

She grinned and walked off.

Mariah ate in silence.

Cam wondered at her spurt of temper and tried to approach conversation from another angle.

"Brian's a cute little kid," he observed. "Resourceful, too. He helped me a lot the night of the flood. Trying to make up for it, I think."

She glanced up at him, her expression softening. She spread jam on a toast point and nodded. "He's a sweetheart. Really a boy—rambunctious and inquisitive and just smart enough to check things out for himself if he wants answers. That's how he got into trouble. He's convinced there's gold stashed somewhere in the carriage house."

"He told me. Said he was going to take the other kids to Disneyland over the summer if he found it." He frowned at her. "I'd have thought kids who are away from their families for most of the year would be eager to go home for the summer. But he filled me in on his mom and Ashley's guardian."

She closed her eyes a moment, thoughts of the children's summer vacations obviously making her even more grim.

So his new conversational gambit hadn't been such a good idea after all.

"It's so sad," she said. "Brian's mother's kind of a flake, and Ashley's guardian intends the best for her but just doesn't know what to do with a little girl. And now he's ill, and she's eventually going to have to adjust to another household."

"Whose?"

"I don't know. Whoever he puts in charge of her care."

"At least the Manor's familiar ground."

That statement seemed to deepen her distress. He was beginning to wonder if he'd lost his social skills altogether.

She put down her piece of toast and said, "The dorm's closing with the school year. They need more room for classes. I think as the Lightfoot sisters get older, maintaining a living space, insurance on the kids, all that day-to-day stuff, is just getting too expensive and worrisome. Letitia just told me this morning."

"I'm sorry." She looked on the verge of tears. He passed her his handkerchief. "Does that mean you're out of a job?"

She stared at the handkerchief in surprise, then up at him. "I didn't think guys carried these anymore."

"Addy gave me a monogrammed twelve-pack for Christmas," he said with a smile. "It's part of her plan to pair up single men and women."

"How so?" she asked, dabbing at her eyes. "Does she intend you to tie a woman to you with them?"

He considered that. "I don't think so, though that does have possibilities. You get weepy, I lend you my handkerchief, you offer to launder it, then we have to get together again so that you can give it back to me. Second date guaranteed."

"I could put it in the mail," she said.

He made a face at her. "Now, that would be just plain obstructive. I'll expect you to find me and return it to me."

She picked up her toast again, took a bite and chewed, clearly working off her dismay over the dorm's closure.

"They'd find another job for me," she said finally, "but I doubt there'll ever be a better time to take my trip."

"How long do you intend to be away?" he asked.

She shrugged, scooping up a bite of omelet. "Until I see no more reason to be there, I guess. Maybe a couple of years."

"Well, then, you may be back just in time to invest in my Chandler Mill project."

"Maybe." She brightened again. "Or maybe I'll have such a good time on my own, answerable to no one, that I'll decide to stay forever."

"So, you never intend to remarry?" Now that she looked relaxed again, he felt safe asking.

"Heavens, no," she denied with quiet vehemence.

He guessed that her obvious determination suggested that she'd been very much in love and therefore very hurt by the divorce.

"The next man you meet might make you happier than your ex did," he said.

"Has nothing to do with that," she replied, studying the toast as though reading something in it. "Time was I could have been happy anywhere."

"What changed?" he asked carefully.

She sighed, put the toast down and sipped at her coffee. "Him," she said finally. "I did, too. And we'd had everything going for us in the beginning. When we failed, I guess I just lost faith in the old dreams.''

''What were they?''

Suddenly Rita appeared to top up their coffees, but when she took in the concerned expressions on their faces, she gave Cam a worried look and moved on.

She shrugged. ''Oh, babies, swing sets in the backyard, Sunday-afternoon drives, August vacations, a big yellow dog.'' She swung her fork in the air as if to erase what she'd just said. ''Doesn't matter. They're gone.''

He found that puzzling. ''But one failed marriage doesn't mean you can't have all those things.''

She looked him in the eye and said with the grimness of someone who'd learned to live with hard facts, ''No, but three miscarriages and a stillbirth do.''

CHAPTER SIX

CAM STARED AT HER in bleak surprise. She wished she'd kept that information to herself. She hated pity. But under the friendly antagonism, he was charming and interested, and all the suppressed details of her life seemed to be forcing their way to the surface.

"It's fine," she said quickly, busying herself with her omelet. "I'm fine. I've adjusted."

"Abandoning your dreams isn't a healthy adjustment," he argued.

"I had little choice. It used to be that I could conceive but never successfully carry a pregnancy. Now even my chances of conceiving are down to one in a hundred.

"What about adoption?"

She could hear all her old arguments with Ben in her head. "My husband wanted his own baby, and I just didn't want to try anymore. And I didn't want another woman to carry it for me."

He didn't ask why she didn't, but she felt obliged to explain.

She stopped eating and laid down her fork. "I

think because I kept trying to get pregnant, even though every miscarriage was devastating. I can't tell you how awful the stillbirth was. I'd finally thought I was going to have a baby, then I stopped feeling movement." She experienced the same tormenting emptiness she'd known when the doctor told her her suspicions were correct and she'd lost the baby. "She was dead. I felt dead. Ben held me and we cried, then he started talking about trying again and I finally realized that while he might have loved me in the beginning, now all our life together meant to him was having a baby. And someone else's baby wouldn't make him happy. It had to be his. And it didn't seem to matter what the effort put me through." Her voice sounded strangled even to her own ears. She took a sip of coffee, then pushed her plate away. "I told him I'd be happy to adopt a baby, but I wasn't going to try again to get pregnant. He said I was being selfish."

Cam remained silent for a moment, then made a sound of exasperation. "Your dreams don't deserve to die because he was a jerk."

"Most men want their own children," she countered. "That's what everyone everywhere has. And that's fine. Maybe you're all entitled. I just don't want to have to deal with it again. I can't have babies, so I've just chosen to go my own way."

He was quiet, simply watched her with an expression that was both sympathetic and disapproving.

To forestall further discussion, she added, "And that's something to which *I'm* entitled."

He finally nodded, pushing his plate away and reaching for his coffee. "You're absolutely right. It's your life, and if your decision is to shortchange it, you have every right to do that. Where do you have to go shopping?"

She opened her mouth to take issue with him, but he'd waved Rita over for the check.

That was fine, she decided. He didn't have to understand. They were just two people having breakfast, going shopping.

"Oh. Almost forgot." Before they slipped out of the booth, he reached two long fingers into the chest pocket of his denim jacket, extracted something and put it in her palm.

Her missing earring! She'd assumed she'd lost it during the flood.

"Thank you," she said. "Where was it?"

"In the middle of my bed," he replied, just as Rita appeared.

Mariah felt the color rise in her cheeks, found herself wanting to explain, then decided against it. Even Parker had been hard-pressed to believe Mariah had thought Cam's dog was killing him and rushed into his bedroom to rescue him.

Cam handed Rita a bill considerably larger than the check required. "Keep the change," he said with a grin, "and your silence, please."

"No, hold on." Rita pocketed the check and bill

and began to stack the plates. "I'll bring your change. I'd much rather be able to talk about what I overheard."

Mariah looked at Cam, uncertain if she was teasing or not.

Cam put his cup and saucer on top of the stack she'd collected and held it there, effectively stopping her tidying.

"Remember when you were making candles and held the dripping form over your sink and managed to seal the drain shut? Who fixed it free of charge because I was there, anyway, to connect your new washer and I had a free afternoon?" He gazed into her eyes. "And you were a little short of ca—"

"Yes!" she said impatiently, anxious to stop him. She glanced around surreptitiously. "I remember."

"Good," he said pleasantly. "Because I'd hate to have to charge you for it."

"I gave you fudge," she whispered.

"I know, and it was delicious. But when you consider that was four or five billable hours…"

"Okay, okay!" she said quietly. "The fact that her earring was in the middle of your bed will never leave my lips." She looked disgruntled. "But that's prime information, you realize. Addy would pay me off in a quilt to know that!"

He smiled. "If I hear a whisper of it anywhere, I'll come after you." He raised his hand from the top of his coffee cup and they grinned at each other.

Mariah couldn't tell if this had been a teasing exchange or his threat was serious.

Rita smiled pleasantly at Mariah. "It was nice to meet you. I understand you have a booth at St. Anthony's Spring Fair." When Mariah appeared surprised, she added, "I'm chairman of the setup committee. I saw your name on the list next to your sister's massage booth. I've wanted one of your signs for a long time." She picked up the stack of plates. "Have a good day, you two." And she walked away.

Mariah was stunned. "Were you teasing her?"

He slipped out of the booth and offered Mariah a hand. "Of course. It was just a reminder that she owes me. She'll be quiet."

Mariah accepted his hand and, grabbing her purse, got to her feet. He retained her hand and led her through the maze of tables to the door. When she caught her trailing purse on the back of an empty chair, she turned to free it and saw Rita standing near the kitchen in the middle of a knot of four waitresses. They were all watching her and Cam and smiling.

CAM WAS FASCINATED as Mariah shopped for the children. The twins needed batteries for their CD players, Ashley wanted styling gel, Jessica had lost the last of her hair clips, Amy and Jalisa begged Mariah to rent the latest Olsen twins movie and Julia wanted Sweet Tarts.

"What are Sweet Tarts?" Cam asked as he carried the bag from the drugstore to the truck. Fred stuck his head inside, searching for treats.

"It's a very sour candy the kids love." She rescued the bag and folded it, intending to keep it on her lap. "Don't let them give you one. It takes a full day to recover."

Cam took it from her and placed it in his storage box in the bed of the truck. He'd had a canopy over the back through the winter and spring, but removed it with the advent of warmer weather.

When he returned to the cab, Mariah was feeding Fred a dog treat. Fred sat up in the middle of the seat, taking the small bites offered him with gentlemanly restraint. When Cam fed him treats, he stood in danger of losing his arm as far as his elbow.

"Where'd you get that?" he asked in surprise.

She smiled at him. Now that they were no longer talking about the past, she seemed comfortable with him. "I bought it from that bin at the counter while you were checking out the *Playboy* magazine."

"I was looking at *Popular Mechanics,*" he corrected her. "You had your back to me."

"I take care of children," she said. "I have eyes in the back of my head."

"Well, you should have them checked. They didn't work when you sloshed coffee all over yourself."

"Who's the centerfold this month?"

"Some pretty little redhead from a Balkan country."

"But you weren't reading it."

"It said so on the cover."

"And you noticed this because *Popular Mechanics* was right next to it?"

"Um, yeah. That's it. Probably placed alphabetically."

His biscuit finished, Fred gave Mariah a large slurp up the side of her face. She giggled and wrapped an arm around the dog as Cam drove off.

At the grocery store, Cam and Mariah split up. He bought anchovies, black olives, salsa-flavored corn chips, a bag of bagels and one of pecan-chocolate-chunk cookies. He picked up a six-pack of Sam Adams beer. When they met near the checkout as planned, Mariah frowned into his cart. "No meat?" she asked.

He shook his head. "I eat out. I just snack at home."

She made a face. "On anchovies?"

"Sometimes I bring a Caesar salad home from the deli. It's not a real Caesar without anchovies, so I put them on myself."

He peered into her cart and saw a colorful, sugary cereal. "Is that good for children?" he challenged.

She held up the box of Cheerios under it. "This is for weekdays with a banana and yogurt. The other is for Saturday mornings so they can have something fun."

"What about the caramel corn?"

She shifted her weight. "That's for the stash I keep in my room." Her direct look into his eyes dared him to criticize.

"In your bedside table?"

"The kids are too smart for that. It's in a hat box in the top of my closet."

He grinned. "Now I know where it is."

She grinned back. "But you're not likely to find yourself in my bedroom, are you?"

He knew she was determined that this attraction could go nowhere, but he hated to turn his back on the possibility.

"Life is filled with the unexpected," he said, falling into line behind her as she wheeled into one of two checkout lines. "Where to after this?"

"The chocolate shop," she replied over her shoulder. "Letty needs raisin clusters. Then the library. I promised Brian I'd try to find a book on the incident at the Manor that led to the story about the gold."

Cam smiled proudly. "He took my advice about needing more research."

Mariah pushed her cart forward as the woman in front of her, groceries paid for, moved on. She began stacking her purchases on the conveyor belt.

"You've become his hero. He drops your name all the time in conversation with the other children. And they're in awe that he got to help you fix the plumbing. You've given him real prestige."

He squeezed by his cart to reach under hers for the flat of two-dozen yogurts she'd stored on the bottom rung. He placed the flat on the conveyor, not sure what to say about her revelation. He'd never been anybody's hero. Well, maybe his little sister's, but that had been a long time ago.

She smiled at his surprise as the clerk continued to scan the contents of her cart. "Does that embarrass you, Cameron?" she asked softly.

He saw a curious sweetness in her eyes over that question and felt an almost uncontrollable urge to kiss her. But he'd already done that once and it had only served to confuse both of them. And after threatening Rita into secrecy, he couldn't very well romance Mariah in the middle of the Maple Hill Market.

So he bluffed it out. "I think it's the forty dollars an hour. I repaired my boss's kitchen sink on Sunday, with the help of his two daughters, and now the youngest one wants to be a plumber. Maybe we should introduce her to Brian. If there's chemistry there, they might grow up to be plumbing moguls."

Her smile deepened, as though she read his mind and his ruse to cover up. Then he got the oddest impression that she wanted to kiss him.

The moment stretched. Their eyes held, her lips parted and she leaned slightly toward him. He felt as if she touched him, drew him toward her.

Then the clerk called out a total—twice—and the

moment was over. Mariah gave the clerk an apologetic smile and wrote a check.

They carried their purchases out to the truck, and Cam put them in the covered box. Mariah leaned her elbows on the bed of the truck and peered in to make sure her two-dozen eggs were carefully placed. Fred stuck his head out the back window, kissing in their direction.

"Do you ever run contraband in there?" she teased. "Illegal aliens? People in witness protection?"

He closed and locked the lid. "No, but I have been known to put smart-mouthed annoyances in it."

She gave him a superior glance and let herself into the passenger side. Fred leaped on her and Cam caught her just as she would have fallen out again. He braced his knee on the running board and propped her up on it.

"I'd better put him in the back," he said, trying to reach around her to open the window all the way so that Fred could get through.

"No, no!" she insisted, wrapping an arm around his neck to steady herself. "He was just being affectionate. He shouldn't be banished for that."

As she spoke the words, their gazes locked and that look from a moment ago was back in her eyes. He couldn't ignore it a second time.

He kissed her with all the conviction he felt that there could be something between them. She seemed to respond with the same belief, a tenderness in her touch, a welcome in her he'd never experienced with a woman before.

Allison had been confident and passionate—qualities he'd appreciated because tenderness had been unknown to him at that point in his life. Other women in his life since then had been eager and daring, almost bold in their attempts to prove that their hearts weren't involved, simply their bodies. He'd be a liar if he said he hadn't appreciated that to a point.

But something about this connection with Mariah was different. He didn't understand it entirely, but he'd never quite connected on this level before—something between all-out passion and uncomplicated intellect.

He wasn't entirely sure what to make of it.

When he finally raised his head, she said breathlessly, "I meant…the dog shouldn't be…banished for it. Not you."

He kissed her again, quickly, just to show her that she couldn't banish what was clearly present and waiting to be explored. Then he put her in her seat, pushing Fred out of the way to make room.

"You can't banish me—I'm driving," he said, then closed the door on her and walked around the truck.

When they came out of the chocolate shop, she handed him a small white bag of chocolate-dipped pretzels. "It's just a thank-you for breakfast," she said offhandedly, "and for making all these stops."

At the library, in the section on local history, they found several diaries of Letitia and Lavinia's great-aunt, Aletha Lightfoot. Mariah tucked them under her arm. "There might be a reference to what happened," she said hopefully.

Cam handed her *A History of Maple Hill, 1858 to 1900.* "This might have a mention, too."

"If Brian rips up the rest of the house," she threatened teasingly, "I'm coming back to get you."

Cam sighed. "I can only hope that happens."

He checked his watch and found that it was almost noon. "Want to go to Perk Avenue for lunch?" he asked.

She opened her mouth to reply, but nothing came out. She was debating the issue with herself, he guessed. He was abjectly disappointed when she said no.

"Back to the Breakfast Barn?" he persisted.

She shook her head again, glancing around in the quiet little library. There were two older people at a worktable toward the middle of the room. Otherwise, they were alone. "I can't, Cam. I have things to do. And…"

He knew what was coming. He didn't want to hear it, intended to ignore it, but she did have the right to say it. He listened patiently.

"We should keep things simple," she said, looking into his eyes with clear reluctance. "I'm going to Europe and you're building your life here. Nothing can come of our attraction. Okay?''

"No," he replied with a smile. She'd admitted attraction. That was important. "First of all, life is never simple, so you can't expect to contain something as far-reaching as love—"

"Love?" she disputed, her voice a little loud. Then she glanced around again, and seeing that they'd disturbed no one, she repeated more quietly, "Love? We—"

"I know." He cut her off before she could build up a head of steam. "It isn't love. We don't know each other well enough. But it's something, and I don't intend to hide from it or try to escape it."

She drew a breath—probably for patience—and firmed her stance, the library books caught in front of her like armor. "Did you hear nothing I said over breakfast?"

He nodded. "I did. It all related to your life with another man. That has nothing to do with us."

"It related to *me*," she corrected him. "Me! The woman's who's lost four babies!"

He nodded again. "I'm sure that was awful, and your husband's reaction to you was brutal. What you're missing here is that I'm not him. I have no problem with adoption. And if we understand this isn't even love yet, why are we even talking about children?"

"Because if it turns out to be," she said, her voice

rising to a desperate whisper, "it'll become an issue!"

"No, it won't. But why don't we wait to have this argument until it turns out to be?"

She faced him stubbornly, and he knew what she was thinking. It *would* turn out to be. So the best thing she could do for herself was keep her distance.

"I think it would be smarter to just save ourselves from that." She dug into her purse, extracted her library card and marched to the desk. He followed and waited patiently while a slender young woman behind the desk scanned the books and handed them across the counter.

Mariah thanked her, then pivoted and walked past Cam as though he wasn't there.

He followed, planning strategy. He wasn't usually good at plots. He was a very straightforward person. But if she was determined to make it difficult, he could do what it took to get the result he wanted.

She waited in front of the locked passenger-side door without looking at him, her chin at a challenging angle.

He ignored her and walked around to his side, unlocking the door. Fred ran at him and he pushed him back into the truck. "Good boy," he said, ruffling the dog's ears. Then he glanced at her over the top of the truck. "Are we holding this relationship together long enough for me to drive you home?" he asked.

She rolled her eyes at him. "Don't be ridiculous, Cam."

"You race into my bedroom," he challenged, "you kiss me as if you've been waiting for me a lifetime—twice—then you claim to read my mind and decide what I do and don't want out of life without even bothering to ask me." He let all that sink in, then asked calmly, "And *I'm* ridiculous?"

She rolled her eyes again, walked around the truck to the driver's door, pushed him aside and climbed in behind the wheel. Fred whined ecstatically as she slid along the bench seat as far as she could.

"Would you please take me home?" she said.

He slipped in behind the wheel and started the motor. With the dog crowding her, Cam didn't have much room to move without touching her—a situation she was trying hard to avoid, considering the way she had her left arm placed across her body to avoid contact.

They were both silent as he pulled out of the parking spot, turned onto Maple Street, then headed out of town toward the Manor.

Mariah's other arm was wrapped around Fred, and the traitorous dog kissed her ear all the way to the school. Cam turned onto the long, maple-lined drive, the trees now bright with small, spring-green leaves. Soon the leaves would be as large as dinner plates. He wondered if Mariah would be gone by then.

He stopped at the junction that led straight to the main building, then made a left toward the carriage house. It was at the top of a slope and had to be approached on foot. He pulled to a stop at the bottom.

Mariah hitched her purse over her shoulder and reached around Fred to push open her door.

"Wait a minute!" he commanded.

She faced him in surprise. Even Fred didn't bolt from the truck as he always did the moment a door opened.

Cam got out, walked around and snapped his fingers for Fred. The dog jumped to the ground and stood right beside him. Cam offered Mariah a hand down. "Just because you insist on being difficult," he said, "doesn't mean that I want to be sloppy. Watch your step."

He unlocked the storage box in the back, retrieved her bags and set them aside in the bed until he had them all out, ignoring her open arms, ready to take them from him. He relocked the box, then gathered up her groceries and other purchases.

"You don't have to..." she began, then stopped when he started up the hill.

She ran around him, Fred following her, and hurried ahead to open the front door. He walked in, through the foyer and past the stairway, still bare of carpet, and into the kitchen. He placed the bags on the large oak table.

She offered her hand, looking uncertain of him.

On one level, he hated that. He'd enjoyed the laughing camaraderie they'd shared at various times throughout the morning. She'd enjoyed his company, and she'd felt safe with him.

But on another level, he guessed, it might be good that she wasn't sure what to make of his reactions. She seemed so sure of her perception of things, wrong as she was, and if she found him unpredictable, it could only help his cause.

He took her hand, keeping his manner casual. Actually, it wasn't what he felt at all. The more time he spent in her company, the more he longed to hold her, kiss her, make love to her so that she would never be able to question what they could mean to each other.

But he had a strategy here. He had to be cool.

"Thank you for a lovely morning," she said. He saw vague disappointment in her eyes. She'd wanted him to kiss her.

"I enjoyed it, too," he replied amiably.

"Thank you for understanding," she added, following him as he walked to the door. Fred hung back, licking at her fingertips.

"I don't understand," he corrected her. "I just refuse to spend valuable time arguing. Goodbye. Come on, Fred."

She said nothing until he was halfway down the slope, then she called, "Thanks again."

He waved and kept going. Fred took several paces back to her but came when Cam called him.

If he stayed away, Cam wondered, would absence make her heart grow fonder? He doubted it, but his choices were slim at the moment.

He opened the passenger-side door to let Fred in, then walked around and got in behind the wheel. Fred looked longingly back at the house and whined.

Cam patted his head. "I know," he said. "Me, too."

CHAPTER SEVEN

SATURDAY NIGHT MARIAH and the children sat around the kitchen table that she'd covered with newspaper and painted some of the signs she would sell at the fair. She'd outlined several with simple designs that would be enhanced, rather than harmed, by less-than-perfect painting.

She'd told the children several days ago about the closure of the Manor's boarding program and their reactions had been surprisingly calm. But she knew sometimes the announcement of major changes in their lives took several days to process. They were just beginning to talk about it among themselves today. She'd thought the painting project would relax them and make them comfortable enough to share their thoughts with her.

"Our mom's coming with her boyfriend to get us when school's over," said Amy, dipping her brush into yellow paint for the center of a stylized daisy on a Bloom Where You Are Planted sign.

"We don't like him." Jalisa painted a blue kitten in the corner of a Quiet—Baby Sleeping sign.

"You haven't even met him, so you don't really

know if you like him or not," Mariah said reasonably. She put clear sealer on several signs she'd painted last night after the children had gone to bed.

"We want her to get undivorced and marry our old dad again." Jessica, her sign finished, dipped her brush desultorily in the water jar and watched it turn colors.

"He got married again to another lady, Jess," Mariah reminded her. "You went to the wedding."

She nodded. "Yeah, but maybe *they'll* get divorced and he and Mom can start all over."

"Uh-uh," Amy said. "'Cause Margie's gonna have a baby." Margie was their father's new wife. "So he has to stay."

"Well, what about us?" Jessica demanded, dropping her brush in the water and sitting back, folding her arms pugnaciously. "How come he didn't have to stay with us?"

"Sometimes married people aren't happy together anymore." Mariah tried to explain the unexplainable. "So they can't live together the way they did before. But that doesn't mean he doesn't still love you. Even if he has another little girl with Margie."

Jessica blew air, clearly disgruntled. "Well, I don't like it."

Ashley, carefully painting the white petals on a daisy, looked up from her work to smile at Jessica. "At least you get to be with your mom. I never get to be with people I know when I'm not at school. And now I can't come back here."

Brian, screwing eye hooks into the tops of the finished signs in order to attach chain, put a finished sign aside and shook his head. "Well, I can't, either, but you don't see me whining about it. I'm going to find the gold and go wherever I want to go."

Ashley leaned her chin on her hand, the paintbrush in her fingers forgotten. "Wouldn't it be cool if that could happen? But where would we go after Disneyland?"

The question seemed to perplex Brian. "We won't go anywhere. We'll just stay there."

"You can't live at Disneyland."

"Why not? They have hotels and stuff."

"I know, but it's a place to play. After you have a vacation, you have to go back to your real life."

He met her gaze with a surprisingly jaded glance for a ten-year-old. "Yeah, but you and me don't have a real life. We live with people hired to take care of us. That's not like having a real life. So I don't see why we'd have to go back to it."

Ashley considered that, and her optimism appeared to dim.

"You're both forgetting how lucky you are that your guardian, Ashley, and your mother's housekeeper, Brian, take good care of you. There are a lot of children in the world whom nobody cares about. That's really sad."

"We have neat parents," Peter said. He clipped chain onto the eye hooks with special, user-friendly hooks Mariah had attached. "We go parasailing in the summer, and waterskiing."

"We jumped out of an airplane last summer!" Philip said.

Mariah shuddered. The Franklins loved their boys, but their idea of fun was daunting to her. The boys, however, were thriving, and Peter, at least, exhibited the same daredevil proclivities their parents had. Philip was less adventurous.

"But it's gonna be weird not to come back here." Peter frowned at his brother. "If we end up in a military school, I'm running away."

"Me, too," Philip seconded.

"Running away never solves anything." Mariah handed a finished sign to Julia, who carried them to the counter where several dozen signs lay to dry. "And I think you're all putting the cart before the horse."

Every pair of eyes looked up at her at the strange metaphor. "Imagine," she proposed, "that Santa's reindeer were behind the sleigh instead of in front of it. What would happen?"

"They'd go backward," Amy said.

Ashley shook her head. "They wouldn't go anywhere. They're supposed to pull."

Mariah nodded, happy to be understood. "So, if you plan for what's going to happen before it happens, you could be all wrong. What you expected to turn out badly might turn out well, but you've already run away, so you'd never know that. You haven't gotten anywhere. You've put the cart before the horse.''

Brian frowned. ''I thought we were talking reindeer and a sleigh.''

She opened her mouth to explain, then caught the laughter in his eyes. He was teasing her.

Ashley sighed. ''Okay, Peter and Philip might end up in a good school, and Jess's mom's boyfriend might be a really neat man, but I don't think Brian and I are going to be surprised. Things are always the same for us. His mom's always gone, and I have all these people I don't know in my life. We have to make some plans.''

She was absolutely right, but Mariah held fast to her plea for caution. ''I'm sure the adults in your life are making plans for you. You don't have to worry.''

Ashley and Brian exchanged a doubtful look and went back to their tasks.

Later that night, after the children were in bed, Parker called.

''I have a new portable chair for the studio,'' she said eagerly. ''Free massage if you want to try it out. I'll bring it over.''

''Only if you want to be showered with chocolate and wine,'' Mariah replied, tugging at the back of her neck where the long nights working on her signs, the stress of worrying about the children and memories of Cameron Trent had all balled into an aching knot. Her sister's healing hands were just what the moment called for.

"Be right there," Parker promised.

They had a glass of wine, shared the quarter pound of Turtles Mariah had bought for herself when she'd shopped for Letitia, and Mariah duly admired the new chair, then sprawled on it to help Parker adjust it.

"Head's just a little high," she said, lifting hers off it so her sister could make the adjustment.

"Try that," Parker advised.

Mariah lay on it again and sank into rapturous comfort. "It's perfect."

"All right!"

Mariah caught the scent of spearmint, violet and roses that Parker had dried herself and sprinkled into her bath. Her sister's hands settled on her shoulders and began to do their work.

"Has he called?" Parker asked, her thumbs kneading Mariah's spine.

Mariah felt herself sink into a level of consciousness once removed from her daily struggle. "Who?" she asked.

"Cam," Parker replied. "Who else?"

"No." Mariah kept her reply simple, unwilling to turn her concentration from the delicious massage.

Though Parker's hands remained firm and apparently focused, her voice took on a suspicious note. "What did you say to him?"

Mariah hesitated before she replied, allowing herself to bask in the comfort of relaxing muscles, knowing that once she answered, the sweetness of this raglike state would be lost.

"You may as well tell me," Parker prompted. "I'm not going away."

"I don't want you to go away." Mariah sighed, her voice vibrating with the strength of the massage. "I just want you to be quiet."

"Fat chance."

Mariah felt the vigorous assault of the sides of Parker's hands across her back from shoulder to shoulder and couldn't help but believe that was some kind of retribution. Even if it did help relax her further.

"I know you saw him on Tuesday," Parker said, working farther down Mariah's back.

Reluctantly, Mariah forced herself to surface from the stress-free depths of comfort. "Did Rita squeal?" she asked, remembering the promise Cam had forced from the woman.

"No." Parker sounded perplexed. "I haven't seen Rita. But Kelly Patrick has a standard Wednesday-afternoon appointment when she gets off work at the Barn."

Mariah had an instant memory of a group of waitresses smiling as they watched her and Cam leave the restaurant.

"She saw the two of you," Parker added.

"I don't even know Kelly Patrick."

"It's Maple Hill," Parker reminded her. "Everyone knows everyone. And we have certain favorites we'd like to see happy.''

''I'm happy.''

''You're lonely.''

''I'm independent.''

''You're trying to escape your loneliness.''

Mariah sat up, annoyed. ''The whole world thinks people are only happy in pairs. I don't happen to agree. And while I appreciate everyone's concern, I'd like it better if they didn't feel obliged to offer advice on my—''

Parker pushed her back onto the chair. ''I'm not the whole world. I'm your sister. And I feel that if you're ever going to be happy, you have to stop living in a box.''

''A box?''

''A box. You've closed your life up so that all you have in it is me and the children.''

''And I'm about to rethink *you!*'' Mariah protested as Parker worked at the back of her waist.

Parker ignored her and continued. ''You're running away to Europe because you believe every man is going to be like Ben, but you're wrong.''

Mariah sat up again, her efforts to relax completely shattered. She fought off Parker's attempt to continue the massage and climbed off the chair. ''I asked Cam what he wanted out of marriage, and he said a loving wife and children.''

Parker spread her arms in exasperation. ''Well, what is so awful about that? Of course he'd want a loving wife and children. But that doesn't mean he'd harass and berate you because you couldn't give him his own. I'm sure if you explained—''

''I did explain.''

''And?''

Mariah turned away from her sister's persistent inquisition and went into the kitchen. She tested the signs and plaques with her index fingertip and, finding them dry, took tissue out of a package she'd opened on a kitchen chair and began to wrap them.

Parker stood beside her, taking the wrapped signs from her and placing them in a box on the floor.

''And,'' Mariah finally replied, ''he said he'd be open to adoption if he found himself in such a situation.''

''Then, what's the problem?''

Mariah sighed and stopped as she prepared to wrap a Quiet—Baby Sleeping sign. It was the one Jalisa had painted with the blue kitten. ''The problem is that Ben and I were in love.'' She held the sign to her and looked into Parker's eyes, remembering how she'd felt when he'd asked her to marry him. She'd been so happy, certain she'd found a lifetime of joy and fulfillment. ''And then I got pregnant, and we were happier than I thought it was possible to be. He was so attentive to me, so loving—as though I was something very precious.''

Parker nodded with understanding, putting a hand on her arm and rubbing gently. ''Then you lost the baby.''

"Yes. Then I lost two more, and by the fourth pregnancy, it was like having our own baby became a matter of honor for him. I felt pain and grief, and he never gave me time for that. He just wanted to try again—to force nature to do what it didn't seem to want to do." Pain filled her chest. It occurred to her that it was like an attack of the heart. "Stephanie had a lovely face, tiny fingers and toes. I held her and got to look at her almost-perfect body, and I just couldn't do it again. Ben held us and cried with me, but started to give me that pep talk I knew by heart. 'I know this is tough, Mariah, but we can't let it defeat us. We were almost successful with this one. We have to try one more time.' And I knew I just couldn't do it."

Parker took the sign from her, put it aside and wrapped her arms around her. "Life makes some people smarter and stronger and others weaker and downright stupid."

"He just wanted his own baby."

"But he wanted it more than he wanted you to be happy. That's not fair."

Mariah pushed her sister away to look into her eyes. "I think maybe it's an instinctive thing, you know? Some impulse or longing placed in men to keep the human race going. A need to see the imprint of your features on future generations, so that the world knows you've been here."

"Yes. That's probably true to a point. But even those impulses have to allow for some exceptions to the rule. Nothing in this world survives without a backup plan. On some level, Ben wasn't man enough to subordinate his ego to your inability to carry a baby to term.''

Mariah nodded grimly. ''The thing is, he'd known me for a long time, lived with me and loved me for four years. We were everything to each other. And he couldn't come to terms with my inability to carry a baby to term. How can I expect another man to be any different?''

''Because you were only everything to each other as long as he thought you could give him what he wanted. When you couldn't, his love evaporated. Makes you wonder if those years you thought were filled with love and happiness really were.''

Mariah sighed, demoralized. ''Makes me wonder if I even have the ability to assess my own life.''

''Of course you do. The fact that he changed on you isn't your fault.''

''Just goes to show you how uncertain love is, anyway. I mean, it's so nebulous to begin with, an emotion dependent upon someone embodying all the things we need in life but can't supply ourselves. We develop this grand feeling for the person because he or she's our other half. But life, time and nature change us, and pretty soon we're not who we were in the beginning. So love dissolves.''

Parker studied her with a frown. ''Well, you paint a pretty bleak picture! I don't think real love does dissolve. I think it makes adjustments.''

"Parker, you've been divorced twice. And you were in love each time you got married."

Parker shifted her weight. "I know. But I fall for needy souls. So whenever I need something, they don't come through for me because they're too busy fending for themselves." She hugged Mariah again. "Are you okay?"

Mariah smiled. "Of course I'm okay."

"Good. Then I'm leaving before you completely disillusion me about love. I still believe in it."

She gathered up her purse and motioned at her massage chair. "And I have a date tomorrow."

"You do?" Mariah picked up the back end of the chair to help Parker out to her station wagon. "Anyone I know?"

"I don't think so. His name is Gary Warren, and he works for Hank Whitcomb, too. He's landscaping my duplex. He's also been coming for massage. He's so easy to talk to."

Hank's men, it seemed, were everywhere. And insinuating themselves into the lives of every woman she knew. She took most of the weight of the chair while Parker unlocked the back of the wagon. Together they pushed in the chair.

Mariah hugged her. "Have a wonderful time and keep believing in everyone and everything as you've always done. Just be on the lookout for selfish qualities and don't let yourself get serious if he has any."

"Right. And you try to be a little more hopeful.

You're helping raise children, remember. You have to make them feel there's hope for the world. Particularly if they're not coming back to you next year.''

Mariah waved her sister off in the darkness, then went back into the house. She wrapped up the remaining signs and packed them into the box, deliberately trying to keep her mind blank.

Cam's face appeared in her mind's eye.

Okay, it was hard to keep her mind blank. But she was not going to indulge it with thoughts of men and love. She would think about her booth.

After several years of doing flea markets, she now had a double-size vinyl pavilion to shelter her wares in case of strong sun or rain. She'd made Peg-Board screens on which to hang the signs, had a card table for doing business and her own cash box. She had to remember to wipe everything off and buy more hooks. Those always seemed to get lost in storage.

She should get a pretty vinyl tablecloth, make a note to pack cold drinks for herself and Parker, and remind Letty and Lavinia that they were watching the children for her.

She also had to remember to go to her storage locker and retrieve a box of signs with Christmas motifs she'd printed two years ago but never sold. She'd ended up in the hospital, losing Stephanie, instead of at the crafts fair the signs had been intended for. And she had to think about something easy for dinner for the children that night.

There. She shook off the pain the thought of one of her babies always brought and congratulated herself on being organized.

The box all packed, she locked the front door, checked the back door, then put the wineglasses and snack plates in the dishwasher. She shut off the downstairs lights and started up to her room.

The house was quiet, the old grandfather clock downstairs ticking its comforting time, the refrigerator humming, the bedsprings creaking as the children turned over in bed.

She hated the prospect of them leaving in two weeks. Since she'd taken over dorm-mother duties last year, her life had revolved around them. The job had been challenging at first, and she'd wondered if God hadn't known what he was doing when he kept her childless.

Then she found her feet with the children, discovered they weren't so much troublemakers as trouble finders, and soon all their qualities, even the ones that kept her on her toes, became very dear to her.

How well they functioned in spite of the turmoil in their lives away from school amazed her.

She found herself wishing she could keep them all with her this summer. Then she realized there would be little point to that if they weren't coming back in the fall.

And anyway, she was going to Europe.

Her mind went instantly to what would happen to

Ashley and Brian. The Morris girls would be fine because their mother loved them and they had each other. The Franklin boys had sunny dispositions and positive attitudes, and parents who always seemed to get away from filming when the boys had a birthday or something special happened.

But Ashley's guardian was dying, and Brian's mother was a flake. Still, as Letty had reminded her, where the children attended school next fall was none of the Manor staff's business.

Mariah wondered if she should call Ashley's guardian and offer to find a good boarding school for the little girl. Letitia would probably discourage it, but she'd have to give it some thought.

She showered, pulled on a cotton nightgown and went to climb into bed, then noticed the light on in her closet. She walked into it, pulled the worn cord to turn the light off and was about to close the closet door, when she heard movement above her head.

She looked up into the closet, a shudder running along her spine. A mouse? she wondered. A raccoon? Letty had told her that they occasionally had a problem with varmints in the carriage house's attic.

She blinked and looked again. It if was a mouse, it must be a particularly clever one, because it had created a large square of blackness where a ceiling tile should have—

She hadn't even completed the thought, when something fairly large glanced off her head and bounced off the clothes rack and into her hands. She screamed, certain it was alive.

Then she felt cold metal and realized it was a flashlight.

That was followed instantly by a cry of alarm and the pitching downward through the hole of hands, arms and a head with cobwebby dark hair.

Mariah reached up instinctively, then she fell to the floor of the closet—along with half her clothes and Brian.

Landing on his back beside her, one foot trapped in the belt of her raincoat, the other caught in one of her shoe pockets tacked to the closet wall, he smiled at her hesitantly, his face smeared with dust.

"You'll be glad to know," he said seriously, "that the gold isn't in the attic."

CHAPTER EIGHT

CAM HELPED EVAN BRAGA assemble the Men's Club booth on the large lawn that usually served as the playground behind St. Anthony's School. Also pressed into service were Hank Whitcomb and his brother-in-law, Bart Megrath. It was very early Saturday morning the first day of the fair, and none of the other vendors had arrived. Jimmy Elliott was baby-sitting Fred for the weekend.

"Wouldn't it be better to buy one of those aluminum things that's easy to carry," Hank asked as he and Bart hauled lumber from Cam's truck to the designated spot in the roped-off area. "And sets up in five minutes?"

"Undoubtedly," Evan replied. He and Cam followed with more pieces. "But an older member of the club provided this booth when his kids were in school, and they've always used it. They see no point in buying some newfangled contraption now." He grinned at his companions. "And that's a quote from the last meeting."

That Evan belonged to this group of older, staid and spiritual men, when church seemed like the last place you'd find him, always amazed Cam. Yet Cam attended regularly.

They had the basic box assembled in half an hour. It was about three times the size of the usual booth.

Cam was about to return to his truck for the slab of wood that would serve as the counter, but Evan loped toward him, waving him back.

"No, we're not going to need that part," he said.

"Won't you want something to rest the food on when you take the money?"

Evan shook his head. "We're not doing food."

"You told me you were making German dogs with peppers."

"Yeah, that's what we usually do, but the wife of one of the men suggested we try something else this year."

Evan went to the open back of Hank's van, pulled out a rolled-up carpet and put it on Cam's shoulder.

Cam balanced it while waiting for Evan to heave a large, plastic-wrapped package out of the rear. "What kind of booth requires a Persian rug?"

"I'm not telling you until it's up."

"But you volunteered me to help in it. I have a right to know what we're doing."

"That's why I'm not telling you. You'll rabbit on me. Come on."

Cam followed him warily across the lawn. "Is it a kissing booth? I'm more open-minded than you think."

"It's not a kissing booth."

"You're not going to dress me in a bra and pass me off as a bearded lady."

Evan laughed. "No. But that's a thought for next year." They walked into the booth through the side left open by the missing counter and Ryan dropped his burden in a corner.

"Just put the rug in the middle. Guys?" he said to Hank and Bart. "Can you get the chairs and the table? Hold on, Cam. The school's janitor is supposed to have left a ladder just inside the front door for us."

Cam unrolled the carpet, and by the time he'd walked over it to settle it into place, Hank and Bart were back with the table and chairs and Evan had an eight-foot ladder.

"The table goes on the rug," Evan directed, "and the chairs on either side. "Cam, want to grab the cabana?"

Cam looked around in confusion. "Cabana?"

Evan pointed to the plastic-wrapped package in the corner.

Cam complied. He removed the contents as Evan climbed the ladder, and discovered it was an old-style beach tent, or cabana, complete with wide blue-and-white stripes and tasseled ornamentation.

Evan threw the heavy fabric over and his companions leaped up to pull it down to fit over the booth. A peaked top rested neatly over the one-by-ones they'd nailed along the top of the booth so that they met in a point in the middle.

"How's it look?" Evan asked from the ladder.

Hank and Bart stepped back to look.

"The point's just a little off center!" Hank shouted. "Pull it to the left. There! Perfect!"

"Looks great!" Bart praised. "You're not jousting or anything, are you?"

Evan climbed down the ladder. "No. We're telling fortunes."

"What?" Cam demanded.

"We're telling fortunes," Evan repeated. "Cam, you're on from eleven to one o'clock, incidentally."

"You told me we were making hot dogs," Cam reminded him. "I have no fortune-telling skills."

"You have no hot-dog-making skills, either," Hank observed. "You burned mine when we watched the game at my house."

Cam drilled him with a look. "That's because your daughter was showing me she could stand on her head and I had to extract her from the recycle box when she fell in."

"We're not claiming to be psychics," Evan said, handing him a large snow globe of a cabin in a cluster of trees near a lake. "It's a carnival game. Here's your crystal ball."

Cam tried to return it. "I can't make up that kind of stuff. People will want their money back."

Cam put it in the middle of the table. "No, they won't. It's a fund-raiser for the school. Will you quit whining? Nobody will expect you to contact their dead relatives or really see into their futures. Just make up something about fame and fortune, and you'll be fine.''

Accepting defeat, Cam told him grimly, ''I can see into your future, buddy, and it isn't pretty. I see traction, around-the-clock nursing care, insurance claims…''

Ignoring him, Evan tacked a sign to the front of the cabana that coaxed, Come Inside For a Message From the Future.''

''I thought churches didn't believe in this sort of stuff.''

''No one's taking it seriously.'' Evan handed him another plastic bag. ''Here're your robes and turban,'' he said. ''You might want to try them on before your shift. Let's go to the bakery. I'm buying.''

Cam clutched the plastic bag to him. ''Turban?'' he asked in horror.

Hank took the bag from him, tossed it onto the table and laughed hysterically as he wrapped an arm around his shoulders and led him back to his truck.

MARIAH HELPED PARKER SET UP her booth—a simple vinyl tent affair bedecked with garlands of silk nasturtiums. Her new massage chair stood in the middle of the small space, and an end table nearby brought from home held her business cards and literature about massage.

When they were finished, Parker helped Mariah

assemble her pavilion, put up the screens, then hang the signs.

"I'll give you a lunch break and watch your booth, if you'll do the same for me," Parker bargained.

"Sure." Mariah delved into the cooler she'd brought and handed her sister a commuter mug containing sweetened iced tea with a slice of lemon. She also handed her a bag of misshapen peanut butter cookies.

Parker bit into one and made a sound of approval. "You and the kids have been baking."

"We have."

"At lunchtime," Parker said, peering out onto the lawn now covered with booths in various stages of construction, people bustling around in their preparations, "St. Anthony's Men's Club usually does German dogs with onions and peppers. They're to die for."

"Sounds wonderful. You can go first, though."

"No, you. All I had to do was lug in the chair. You had all kinds of stuff to get ready. Oops. Got a live one." A young woman stood inside Parker's booth, studying the handout. "Thanks for the tea and cookies."

"Sure."

Mariah had sold a fourth of her stock by eleven o'clock.

She was rearranging signs to close up bare spots,

when Letitia and Lavinia walked by, the children clustered around them.

Ashley noticed immediately that some of the stock had been sold. She pointed to a large sign Mariah had painted herself and placed at the top. It read Live Well, Laugh Often, Love Much. "That's my favorite. I wonder why nobody's bought it yet?"

"I'm sure it's waiting for just the right person," Mariah replied. "We'll divvy up the money you all made today," she told the group, "so you'll have extra money to spend when you come back tomorrow."

"After lunch," Ashley said excitedly, "I'm going to have my fortune told."

"I'm going to buy a candy apple!" Julia said.

"I'm going to play the Wheel of Fortune." Brian held up two one-dollar bills. "It only costs fifty cents, and the girls win dolls and the boys get trucks."

"All right! What do the adults get?"

He shrugged. "I don't know. Probably books, or something." She guessed that was the dullest thing he could think of.

"Well, let's move on and see if we can find the cakewalk," Lavinia proposed. "I'd love to win a chocolate cake."

"A wish I applaud," Letitia said, shooing the children before them. "Good luck, Mariah. We'll see you at closing time."

Mariah waved as they started away and several young girls wandered into her booth, giggling.

She'd picked the top-twenty girls names out of a baby book and made several for each, some with butterflies, some with flowers and some with kittens. She sold two Sarahs, a Brittany and a Bailey.

In addition to the children earning money, she realized, checking the contents of her cash box, her European trip account was doing well.

She was famished when Parker appeared to relieve her at just after noon.

"You're sure you want me to go first?" she asked. "I know you've been really busy, too. Your hands must be aching."

Parker flexed them happily. "They're used to this. And I've signed up three new regular weekly customers. Go ahead. I'll be fine."

"Okay. I'm starved." Mariah grabbed her purse from under a folding chair and took off down the fair's lively midway.

Her first stop was a booth with handcrafted jewelry. She found a necklace made of silver beads she knew Parker would love, admired a star-shaped brooch for herself, then decided against it, opting to put the money in her Europe fund, instead.

She pitched pennies and played the ring toss to no avail, but joined in the cakewalk and won a butter brickle cake. The children, she knew, would be thrilled to have it for dessert tonight.

She carried the cake to her car, delivered the

necklace to Parker, who gave her a squeal of delight and a big hug, then continued on her way. She signed up for a quilt raffle and was getting serious about finding something to eat, when she noticed the striped tent and the invitation to Come Inside for a Message From the Future.

She wasn't sure why that intrigued her, but it did. Gypsies with bangle bracelets and wild eyes had always fascinated her. She parted the striped folds and peered in. It would be fun to pretend that there was some mystery about her future.

CAM WAS MAKING a bundle for the Men's Club. He'd told a dozen fortunes and was beginning to feel comfortable with his turban and Hungarian accent. The face-enveloping beard and mustache, however, must have been made of something smelly and flea-bitten. He was continually having to scratch under it.

He was wondering if fortune-telling could be a lateral career move from plumbing, when a familiar dark head peeked inside the tent. His first thought was that Mariah knew he was working the booth and had stopped by to say hello, or to remind him that she didn't want to see him again.

But he realized as she looked around and stepped hesitantly inside that she had no idea who was under the robe and behind the thick, dark beard.

She peered at him, hesitated, appearing to consider a hasty exit.

"Come in, Princess," he said with a thick roll of *R*s and the slur of consonants that seemed to give him some authenticity, if not exactly credibility.

She peered around again.

"I was expecting a Gypsy," she said. She wore jeans that clung to her flat stomach and slender limbs, and a white blouse with pink roses. Her hair was caught up in a loose knot, bangs fringing her forehead. She looked very young; nothing about her indicated all she'd been through in life.

"I am son of Othar, prince of the Gypsies," he said, beckoning her toward the table with an index finger bejeweled with a ring probably taken from a bubble gum machine. It, and the other three he wore, had come with the costume. "Come, Princess."

She took several more steps to the table, smiling. "I meant a Gypsy *woman*."

"Ah," he said, sweeping a hand toward the chair. "In my family, the gift of prophecy is passed from father to son. The women are not quiet long enough to hear the stirrings of dreams."

She sat down, leaning forward and smiling. "And how do you hear them?"

He made a broad gesture upward with his hands. "They're in the snow."

"Well…" She pointed to the sun streaming through the open slit of tent. "It's May, Gypsy prince. Almost June."

He framed the globe in front of him with his hands, passed them over it as though casting a spell, then picked it up in one hand, spun it theatrically, then placed it right side up on the table. Snow swirled like a blizzard inside it.

"In my tent," he said softly, "it is only…the future!" He added the last two words in a dramatic whisper.

"Yes, well. Here's my five dollars." She put a bill on the table. "Your sign says that gets me a message from…the future!" She repeated those two words with the same whispered note he'd used.

"I see…" He leaned closer, narrowing his gaze on the globe as if having difficulty reading it. "I see…children."

"Yes," she said. "There are children in my present life. Are you one of the Manor's parents?"

He cupped his hands around the globe without touching it. "No, this is the *future*. There are children in your *future*. A yellow cottage with climbing roses on the picket fence."

He chanced a glance up at her and saw her staring at him. Had she forgotten he was in a role?

Had he? He found himself wanting to give her back her dreams.

"Ah!" he said.

"What?"

"A ship."

She hesitated a moment, then asked with bald cynicism, "I'm going into the merchant marines?"

He frowned over the globe. "No. You are a passenger."

"Oh. A Caribbean vacation?"

"No. I see you at the Louvre, the Prado, the National Gallery."

He heard her intake of breath, and wondered if he'd gone too far. Thinking that if he had, he may as well go for broke, he continued. "Later, you will meet a handsome stranger. Together you will find the yellow cottage and the children. You will have an easel in a room with a dormer window facing north. It looks out on swings in a backyard, a yellow dog."

She stared at him in silence, a dreamy wonder in her eyes. As he watched, her expression hardened to suspicion.

MARIAH FELT HERSELF inhale his message from the future like oxygen. She took it into her lungs, into her bloodstream, willing to believe in this blue-and-white tent with a snow globe for a crystal ball and a playful Gypsy charlatan across the table and that he was telling her the truth.

How could he have known? she asked herself as she tried to get a grip, tried to reason this through. A few people were aware she planned a trip to Europe, but not many knew she was going on a self-conducted art tour—just Parker and the Lightfoot sisters. And the swings and the yellow…

Reality fell on her like an anvil. She stood and reached across the table, yanked on the bristly beard and slapped off the turban. She looked into a roughly handsome face with hazel eyes. "Cameron Trent! You...you liar!"

"I wasn't lying, Mariah," he denied. "I was indulging your dreams. You should be doing that for yourself."

He reached a hand out toward her and she batted it away angrily. "Don't try to talk around it! You pretended to be someone else and used what you knew about me to...to..."

"Give you your five dollars' worth?" he finished for her. He folded his arms and wisely kept his distance.

She was furious. She had a vague misgiving about why she should be so upset about a fortune-telling booth clearly intended as harmless entertainment, but she was too angry to be rational.

"Five bucks for a dream?" he added. "Cheap at twice the price."

She snatched up her five dollars and jammed it into the side pocket of her jeans. "I'm taking my money back. I thought you were supposed to be cooking hot dogs for the Men's Club."

"They changed their minds about what they wanted to do."

"Well, I think you should have stuck to food!" She knew she was being ridiculous, could see that in his eyes. Unable to explain or defend herself, she pivoted to leave.

Strong fingers manacled her wrist and turned her to face him.

"Do you even know why you're so upset about this?" he asked.

She tried to yank free, unwilling to discuss it.

He held firm. "Because my phony glimpse into the future, tailored to what I know you want, reminded you that you do still believe in your dreams. And Europe isn't the only thing you want. You want the handsome stranger, the cottage and the children. You bought into it because you believe."

She opened her mouth to remind him that she couldn't have children. He seemed to read her mind and interrupted with, "Adopted children, foster children. Any kind of children."

"Let me go," she demanded coldly.

He did.

She slapped the five dollars back into his hand, reminding herself that it was for the school, then she hurried out. She ran into Letitia and Lavinia and the children, who all had corn dogs and pizza and invited her to join them. What she really wanted to do was run to her car, but she drew a deep breath, instead, noticed a family of six leaving one of the many picnic tables set up near the playground equipment and ushered everyone in that direction.

"Are you all right, dear?" Lavinia asked solicitously.

She smiled, nodded and swallowed the barbed anger she felt at the discovery that she did still want all those things she'd turned her back on. Which was insane, because all the effort to acquire them did was cause her pain.

She really could have slugged the phony Gypsy prince for reminding her of it.

CERTAIN HE'D JUST RUINED whatever fragment of chance remained that he could make a friend of Mariah Mercer, Cam put his beard back on, dusted off his turban and placed it on his head. Then he resumed his chair, tipped the snow globe on its head and righted it again, looking for his own future in it. He saw nothing in the lonely little cabin near the woods. And maybe that was prophetic, he thought unhappily.

He spotted a smudge on the glass, and as he rubbed it off with the sleeve of his robe, he heard the quiet clearing of a throat. He looked up to see Ashley standing just inside the door. She wore blue cotton pants and a white shirt with three little blue hearts on the pocket. A little white purse dangled from her shoulder. Her blond hair was pulled into one neat French braid. He wondered if Mariah had done it.

"Can you tell my fortune?" she asked eagerly.

He remembered what Mariah had mentioned about her, and felt a sudden sense of panic. He couldn't deny her, but he would have to handle this carefully. After the disaster with Mariah, he doubted his ability to do so.

"Yes, I can," he said. "Come in and sit down."

She opened her purse with distinctly feminine movements, then handed him a five-dollar bill. He gave her four dollars change.

"The sign says five dollars," she pointed out.

He nodded. "But we have a special rate for children because…ah…because they're smaller."

Her brow wrinkled. "It should cost more for children because there's more of a future for you to see."

After that astute observation, he doubted his ability to put anything over on her.

"I'm at kind of a crossroads," she said seriously, like one adult to another.

He listened intently. "I see."

"I've had a guardian since my parents died," she said, "and I don't see him very often. Everyone's trying to keep it a secret, but he's sick. He's going to die."

Cam did his best to remain in character. "I'm sorry."

"Yes, I am, too. Not that I ever got to spend much time with him. He couldn't really decide what to do with me."

Cam felt sorry for the unknown guardian. What was there to know about dealing with such a beautiful, precocious little girl? She sounded as though she'd have been grateful for any attention.

"What I was wondering about," she continued, leaning toward him conversationally, "is if you can see me getting new parents."

The question rendered him momentarily speechless.

"The Manor isn't taking boarding students next year, so when I leave at the end of next week, I won't be coming back. So..." She shrugged bony little shoulders in an artless acceptance of fate. "I wondered if I was going to get real parents, since I can't pretend to be Mariah's daughter anymore." She leaned forward to peer into the ball and asked, "How does that work, anyway? Can I see things, or just you?"

"Well..." He forced himself to try to analyze how best to reply. He could promise nothing, but there had to be a way he could give her hope. "Sometimes I see things," he said, tipping the ball, then righting it again. "And sometimes I don't. The ball usually only works for the one who owns it." That was probably Gypsy fortune-telling heresy—he wasn't sure.

"It's not a crystal ball." She expressed that as an observation rather than an accusation. "It's a snow globe."

"I read things in the snow," he replied, wondering if his crystal ball was the only thing she could see through.

But she seemed to accept that and settled down to listen.

"I see..." He thought frantically. "I see success in your future," he said. "You have a briefcase."

She frowned again. "I want to be a ballerina."

"Well…a successful ballerina will have a stock portfolio, appointments, fan mail to reply to." He looked up to smile at her. "And she might keep her ballet slippers in her briefcase."

Ashley giggled, liking that notion. "What else?" she asked, sitting forward.

"I see audiences applauding," he said, "and ballet companies fighting over you. And do you know why?"

Her blue eyes were wide with curiosity. "Why?"

"Because you've studied and worked so hard to learn to dance and to conduct your own business that you're the best dancer in the world. You're a self-made woman."

"What does that mean?"

"That you did it on your own. That it wasn't because you had all kinds of people working for you. It was because you knew what you had to do to be good, and you did it."

She thought about that a moment, seemed undecided about whether it was good or bad, then asked with a disappointed wince, "So I'm not getting the parents?"

He looked her in the eye. "I can't see whether you do or not. It doesn't mean you won't, just that I can't see it. All I can tell you for sure is that you're going to grow up to be a woman who makes her own future."

"By studying hard."

"Yes. By figuring out what has to be done and doing it."

She considered that, then nodded. "By taking responsibility. Mariah always talks to us about that."

"She's right. And taking responsibility for your own life is the smartest thing you can do."

She agreed, yet appeared to remain somewhat dissatisfied. She reached for the globe, turned it over, shook it, then put it back on the table. "Would you look one more time?" she asked hopefully. "Just in case? Even parents with another kid would be good 'cause then I'd have a sister. Or a brother. A sister would be better, though. Do you see it?"

He looked closely until the snow settled, a pain in his heart for the wish he couldn't promise, the right every child should be able to count on.

He steeled himself and met her longing gaze. "I'm sorry," he said. "I can't see it. Remember that it doesn't mean you won't have it, just that I can't see it."

"How come," she asked politely, "you can see some things and not others?"

Good question. He sought frantically for an answer. "That's a mystery to me, too," he said finally. "It could be that the energy in the air today just isn't letting it come through." That sounded lame, even to him.

But the trusting little girl believed him. His heart ached even more.

She stood and pushed her chair up to the table as

Mariah had taught the children to do in the kitchen at the carriage house. "Thank you very much," she said. "At least I know I'll be a ballerina because I'm going to work hard."

"That's right. Good luck, Ashley."

She turned on her way to the tent flap, her eyes wide. "You saw my name?"

"Yes, I did," he replied.

She took a step back toward him. "What's my last name?"

He couldn't remember if he'd ever heard it. He shook his head. "I didn't see that."

"Oh." She smiled. "That's okay. I thought if it was different from what it is now, I'd know if I was going to get parents. Bye."

"Bye." He watched the tent flap close as she disappeared, then collapsed into his chair. That interview had taken every nerve he possessed and tied it in a knot. How could a child like that not have everything she wanted? What kind of a world was it, anyway? He wanted answers.

The thought had no sooner formed than the tent flap opened again and Father Chabot, pastor of St. Anthony's, walked in with a five-dollar bill, which he slapped on the table in front of Cam.

"Do the Sox have a chance at the pennant this year or not?" The priest, a rotund, habitually cheerful man, sat across from him in everyday garb of slacks and plaid shirt.

Cam was sure the priest knew his identity. He had

helped him with church projects and had dinner in the rectory on several occasions.

Cam worked his hands over the globe. "I can see it wouldn't be wise to put money on it, Father."

The priest laughed. "Your salvation's in jeopardy, son," he said.

Cam didn't have to look into the ball to know that was true.

CHAPTER NINE

MARIAH NOTICED THAT Ashley was pensive at dinner. While the other children happily devoured the cake Mariah had won, Ashley played with her piece, decorating the frosting with the tines of her fork.

"Don't like butter brickle?" Mariah asked.

Ashley sighed. "I guess I'm full."

Mariah put a hand diagnostically to the child's cheek. "Do you feel all right?"

"Yeah." Ashley pushed her plate away and took a long pull on her milk. She daintily wiped away the resultant milk mustache with her napkin. "Did you know," she asked, leaning back in her chair, "that you can make your life turn out any way you want it to?"

Mariah ignored the instinct to answer with a qualifier, deciding that life would do that soon enough without any help from her. The best thing she could do was strengthen Ashley's belief in that premise.

"Yes, I did."

"Do you know how to do it?"

Mariah smiled. Talking with children was always full of booby traps. "Um, I think you do it by studying hard so that you understand how things work, then by working hard so that you can get things done.''

Ashley smiled, clearly delighted that she grasped the concept. "And by never giving up. Because if things get bad, you might be able to fix it if you're trying, but if you're not, then nothing good can happen.''

Mariah nodded her approval, wondering where this philosophical thought had come from.

"Did you come to understand this all by yourself?" she asked.

Ashley shook her head. "The fortune-teller told me.''

Mariah's heart punched her in the ribs. "He did?"

Ashley nodded, her right leg swinging as she reached for her milk again. She took a sip, then put the glass back, running her index finger along the stem of a flower decorating the side. "He couldn't tell me if I'm going to get parents, though.''

Before Mariah could recover from her surprise at that statement, Ashley added with a very adult acceptance, "I know Mr. Kerwin is sick, and pretty soon he'll have to give me to someone else.''

Mariah opened her mouth, wanting to offer all kinds of assurances that the man had her best interests at heart and would find her a wonderful family. But she knew she couldn't promise that. She was sure he cared about Ashley, but he also seemed to have little clue about what she needed.

"He also couldn't see whether I'm going to get a brother or a sister if I get a family."

"No. I imagine that would be hard to predict." Mariah tried to revive the anger she'd felt after her "reading" with Cam; however, the good advice he'd given Ashley made it impossible. "But you understand that the fortune-teller was just pretending. I mean, he wasn't really able to predict the future. He was just one of the men from St. Anthony's in a robe and a turban, trying to make money for the school. Just like all the other games at the fair."

Ashley sat up and leaned earnestly toward her. "No, I believed him. And he didn't tell me any lies. He said sometimes he can see stuff and sometimes he can't."

Mariah didn't want to do anything to diminish the good message Ashley had gotten out of the experience, but she felt called upon to repeat, "That was probably because he can't really do it. He was just pretending to help the school make money."

Ashley shook her head. "It's because sometimes the energy can't come through the air, or something."

"Really."

"It doesn't mean I won't get them," Ashley said, sounding hopeful. "Just that he can't see it. But he could tell that I'll get all the other stuff I want—like be a ballerina—if I take responsibility for my life. Just like you always say."

"Right," Mariah had to agree. "How much did he charge you?" she asked, wanting something to use against Cam for his using her dreams against her.

"Just a dollar," Ashley replied. "I told him I thought kids should be more expensive 'cause they have a bigger future to look into, but he said no. They get a deal 'cause they're kids."

"He did."

"Yeah." Ashley pulled her cake toward her and picked up her fork to attack it with new vigor.

"So, I'm going to believe that I'm gonna get parents, and maybe a sister, and when I grow up, I'm gonna be a ballerina." Ashley popped a forkful of cake into her mouth and chewed, nodding to herself as though everything she'd just explained to Mariah was settling inside her like a truth.

So. Cameron Trent had given Ashley hope—a valuable gift. Mariah gathered up the dishes, trying not to think about him. All he'd tried to do was give her hope, just as he'd done for Ashley, so it was hard to stay angry. But she'd been around long enough to know that even the most stalwart determination to achieve a particular goal could be thwarted by insurmountable facts. She'd given up on her dreams. It had been painful to discover they apparently hadn't given up on her.

She put a Disney movie in the DVD player and the children sprawled on the floor to watch.

Only Brian held back, lingering at the table over a second glass of milk.

"Tired?" Mariah asked, filling the dishwasher. "I hear you and the twins sank so many baskets at the free-throw booth that all the girls were after you for the stuffed animals you won."

He nodded, a wistful smile on his lips. "I'm gonna miss this kind of stuff. At home, every-thing's..." He shrugged, having difficulty express-ing himself. "I don't know. Big. Fancy. They do a lot of stuff and it's for charity, too, but if we go, we always have to get dressed up and smile for the cam-eras and my mom talks to reporters or other actors. I usually walk around by myself and wish I was here, instead, where it's small and friendly."

Mariah's heart ached for him. She went to sit be-side him and gave him the last piece of cake. "I know what you mean. Sometimes I feel out of place at parties." Baby showers, particularly. Or chil-dren's birthday parties. "But it doesn't usually last very long. And chances are your mom will look for another small private school like this one, where they'll do a lot of the small-town things we do here."

He gave her a skeptical look, then leaned back in his chair and studied the cupboards. "These cabinets aren't that old. I wonder if the gold's behind them."

THE SECOND DAY OF THE spring fair dawned sunny and warm, and the children were up early, looking forward to another day of playing games and eating junk food. Mariah had to admit that she wouldn't mind a second plate of curly fries herself.

She divided the cash earned from the signs they'd helped with and distributed it among them.

The Lightfoot sisters again took the children for the day so that Mariah could man her booth. She restocked her display, delighted by the number of signs she'd sold. She'd even dug out her Christmas stock, knowing that for some shoppers, it was never too early.

Parker leaned around the corner of her booth to hand her a paper cup with a lid. "Mocha," she said. "Figured I owe you for the iced tea yesterday. Want a muffin? I've got those sour cream-blueberry ones from Perk Avenue."

"Yum." Mariah left her booth to step into Parker's. It was time for the fair to open, but the real crowd wouldn't arrive until after the ten-thirty mass—another five minutes.

Parker handed Mariah a muffin in a little white box, a golf-ball-size dollop of whipped butter included. Her sister appeared a bit flushed this morning, Mariah thought as she dug into a paper bag for napkins and plastic forks. They sat on two folding chairs Parker had placed against the side of her booth.

"You look a little…" Mariah tried to analyze her sister's expression.

Parker glanced at her, then away, obviously embarrassed. Mariah watched her in surprise, thinking that Parker was usually so open about her thoughts and behavior that nothing gave her pause.

Then Parker stared her right in the eye and seemed unable to stop smiling. Mariah remembered she'd had a date.

"He was Mel Gibson in disguise?" Mariah guessed playfully.

Parker giggled. "Better than that. He was just Gary Warren."

"Ah." Mariah found herself smiling, too. "It went well?"

Parker took a bite of muffin and chewed slowly, clearly buying time. Mariah waited patiently.

Parker looked into Mariah's eyes again and this time flushed bright red. "He is the nicest, dearest, sexiest man I have ever met. I'm in love."

Mariah felt obliged to ask, "Park, does he have his own money?"

"He does landscaping and gardening for Whitcomb's Wonders—I told you that."

Mariah nodded. "Why doesn't he go out on his own?"

"Because he has two teenagers, and Hank's willing to schedule him so that he can be around for them. But they'll both be in Europe for the month of June—one of those school-exchange things." She smiled again, then just as quickly frowned. "They were very polite, but it was hard to tell if they liked me or not."

Mariah made a face at her. "How could anyone not like you? Where's their mother?"

"Died five years ago of a heart attack. She'd always been frail. Mariah." Parker's eyes grew wide with the intensity of her feelings. "I know my track record is questionable, but he's so...special! And— miracle of miracles—he thinks I am, too."

Mariah wrapped her left arm around her, careful of the mocha she held in that hand. "Only because you are. I'm excited for you, sis, but...you know. Be careful. It's a little early yet, and two teenagers— I mean, that's major lifestyle adjustment."

Mariah sighed. "U-huh. I'm trying to keep a cool head. But you know how I am about love. It just fills me up and spills over and I want to give everyone everything." Before Mariah could suggest caution again, Parker cut her off with a vigorous nod. "I've managed to be interested but calm. Even when he told me he loved me, I kept my feelings to myself. I told him we'd only dated once, even though we've known each other for months and talk about important things all the time."

"He told you he loved you?"

Parker blushed anew. "He was very firm about it. He said he's watched me for months and was sure someone younger and richer would snap me up." She wrinkled her nose. "Isn't that cute?"

Mariah had to nod, unable to cast a shadow on her delight. "Very cute. When are you seeing him again?"

"Tonight," Parker replied. "He and the kids are coming here this afternoon, then we're going to the fried chicken dinner in the parish hall."

"Oh!" Mariah was meeting Letitia, Lavinia and the children there. "Then you can introduce me." She had to see this paragon for herself. Parker was simply not trustworthy where men were concerned. By her own admission, she fell in love quickly and hard, only to wake up a year or two later alone and disillusioned—and broke!

The church bell rang, and within minutes the crowd began to thicken. Mariah closed the box on the half muffin remaining, swallowed her last sip of mocha and gave Parker a supportive hug. "Good luck today," she said.

Mariah went back to her booth, where she did a brisk business, even selling more of her Christmas signs. It was midafternoon before things slowed down.

Parker peered around the corner, her expression pleading. "If you watch my booth for a few minutes, I'll go find us something for lunch."

Parker had taught her the basics of massage, but her sister had a rare touch. "You brought breakfast. I should buy lunch."

"No, no. The choir mothers are selling German dogs. Doesn't that sound good?"

"Yes. And you want to share a plate of curly fries?"

"Absolutely."

Mariah reached for her purse, but Parker was gone before she could dig out her wallet. She pinned the curtains back between their booths with a large clothespin so that she could move easily from one to the other.

There was no action in her booth, so she occupied herself by straightening her display. She had only half a dozen signs left—two longer, and therefore more expensive, ones; two Christmas signs encouraging snow; and two signs the children had helped with.

She heard a throat clear behind her and turned, a welcoming smile on her face—to see Cam standing next to Parker's massage chair.

CAM HAD NEVER MET a woman who could kill a smile as quickly as Mariah could. He ignored her sudden frown and said politely, "I have a two-thirty appointment."

"Parker hasn't been making appointments here," she said.

"She did for me," he insisted.

"Well, she's gone for about fifteen minutes," she replied, equally polite, if a little stiff.

He glanced at his watch. "I'm supposed to be at city hall in half an hour. Some problem in a bath-room on the second floor."

Her eyes went to the ten-dollar bill in his hand and devotion to her sister apparently overtook her unwillingness to help him. He had to give himself credit for that. From across the midway, he'd seen her watching both booths and guessed waving cash around—cash her sister could use—might earn him a little one-on-one with her. She made him nuts when he wasn't with her; he might as well go for stark-raving mad when he was.

She took the ten from him, spread a clean towel on the top of a chair that looked like some exotic bicycle without wheels and beckoned him to it.

He knelt astride it, waiting for it to collapse under him. Mercifully, it didn't.

She patted the little shelf where she'd place the towel. "Rest your head here."

He made a production of looking up and around. "Is there a blade that's going to come down from somewhere and behead me?"

He could see that she wanted to smile but wouldn't give him the satisfaction.

"If you have an appointment, we really don't have time for comedy, do we?"

"There's always time for comedy," he said, placing his right cheek on the towel. "Some of us have just forgotten how to laugh. Stay off my ribs. I'm ticklish."

Something changed inside him the moment her fingertips touched him. He'd tried to be hopeful and positive despite his childhood and the Allison experience, but he knew old grudges had hidden in corners, gotten lost inside with old memories.

Mariah's hands in the middle of his back, between his shoulder blades, seemed to touch those places. He knew it was probably wishful thinking on his part. Old injuries didn't simply disappear under the hands of a woman who didn't even like him—even though he wanted to think she did. But as her hands worked over him in firm but gentle circles, he swore he felt edges soften inside him, barbs being smoothed away.

"Why didn't you go into massage, too?" he asked. His mind was trying to put another spin on this experience, and he had to keep talking to distract himself. He could remember her in the middle of his bed, and the long strokes of her hands down his sides now made him wonder how they'd feel without the barrier of a shirt. "Wouldn't it be easier than taking care of children?"

"Life's not supposed to be about doing the easy thing," she said, leaning into the massage. Her touch was now almost punitive. "You made that pretty clear to Ashley, Gypsy prince, son of Othar."

"She's a beautiful little girl," he said, preparing to defend himself for his "reading" to her. "And I didn't promise her anything. I just—"

"She told me all about it," she interrupted. He felt her knuckles under his shoulder blades. "You told her she was in control of her own life and that she'd get what she wanted if she worked hard for it. That was very good advice."

He sat up with a hand to his heart and she stood back worriedly. "What? Oh, God, did I hurt something? A rib? I know how to do this, but I push too—"

He caught her wrist to stop her. "Did you just compliment me?" he asked.

She expelled a breath and rolled her eyes, clearly relieved that he wasn't injured. He allowed himself to be flattered by that.

"I believe I did," she admitted, pushing on his shoulders until his cheek was on the towel. "But that doesn't mean anything. I'm sure I'll be completely annoyed with you again any time now."

"I'm sorry about your reading," he said quietly as she worked down his spinal column with gentle pressure. "I didn't mean to embarrass you, just to…give you your dreams."

A sturdy blow struck his right shoulder. He guessed it was more therapeutic for her than for him. "That isn't within your power to do," she said.

"Maybe it is."

A similar blow struck his left shoulder. "I'm telling you it's not. There. Finished."

He sat up, rubbing a hand where that last blow had landed. Now he was annoyed. Her touch was so delicious. How could her brain be so out of sync with it?

"You know, just because you spend your days

telling little children what they can and can't do,'' he said, ''you shouldn't delude yourself into thinking it works with me.''

She blinked at him in mild surprise, taking a step backward when he stood.

He stepped toward her. ''You're not the only one who's had your dreams ripped out of you, you know. But they're plans for tomorrow, and if you let them go or let them die, then you go backward. There's no standing still in life. Time keeps moving.''

She stared at him, apparently trying to decide between anger at his presumption and acceptance of the truth of what he'd said. He should have known which she'd choose.

She put on a haughty expression and tapped the face of her watch. ''Then you should be moving on to city hall.''

Now really annoyed, he caught her wrist and hauled her with him into her booth.

''What do you think you're doing?'' she demanded, trying to yank free of him. He held on.

''Buying a sign,'' he said, reaching for a long one he'd admired several times as he'd walked by unnoticed. Live Well, Laugh Often, Love Much, it read. It had made him decide to buy Hank's house.

He finally freed her hand to reach for his wallet.

She wrapped the sign in tissue and thrust it at him.

He handed her several bills.

''Thank you,'' she said stiffly.

"You're welcome," he replied. "Will you have dinner with me tonight in the parish hall?"

He asked her simply to torture himself. When things were impossible, he loved to push them just a little further to show himself he could survive.

"I'm meeting the Lightfoot sisters and the children there." Her arms were folded belligerently, but there was a different message in her eyes. One she probably understood no better than he did. He was considering whether to accept her rejection or suggest another time and place, when she said with an almost defiant squaring of her shoulders, "You can sit with us."

It took him a second to get over the initial shock, then he nodded casually. "Good. I'll be by for you at closing."

"Fine."

He was afraid to think of this as progress, but he couldn't help it. God. He was turning into an optimist!

PARKER RUSHED INTO the booth holding two paper trays containing German dogs with sauerkraut and curly fries with ketchup. She stopped just inside the booth to frown at her sister. "What happened?" she demanded. "Your cheeks are purple."

"Nothing happened," Mariah replied calmly, taking one of the trays. "But if you're going to make appointments to give massages, you shouldn't walk away for fifteen minutes when one is due. Did you bring drinks?''

''I didn't make any appointments.'' Parker turned sideways so that Mariah could see the can of soda protruding from the pocket of her slacks. ''What are you talking about?''

Mariah fell into one of the folding chairs, rested the tray in her lap and popped the top on her can of diet cola. She had to do something about that man. ''Cam said he had a two-thirty appointment with you. I had to do the massage because he couldn't wait until you got back. He had a job.''

Parker raised an eyebrow at her gullibility. ''And you think I'm the one with no defenses.'' She grinned before taking a bite of curly fry. ''I walked right past him when I went to find our lunch. He knew I was gone.''

Mariah really wanted to be angry. But all she could remember was the warm, tight muscle under her hands, the sturdy structure of his back and shoulders, the impulse to lean against him and close her eyes that she'd almost succumbed to.

She didn't know why she had invited him to join their table tonight. Her mind, which had once been very organized and determined, was now muddled and wishy-washy. She hated that.

''He's joining me and the kids and Letitia and Lavinia tonight at the dinner. Why don't you and Gary Warren and his kids sit with us?'' She felt the need for reinforcements. ''I promise not to cramp your style. You can go off together as soon as dinner's over. I imagine his kids will be staying for the rock band in the gym.''

Parker smiled widely, her expression one of longing. ''That'd be great. When things were crazy with Mom and Dad and we were stuck out on the farm, even though I loved the life, I was a young teenager and sure I'd never meet anybody.''

Mariah tried to relate that information to their present conversation and couldn't quite do it.

Parker put her cold can of soda to her cheek as she stared ahead of her. ''And I wanted so much to meet someone. I wanted to get married and have children so that when you got married, I'd already have a house with a big yard and we could all have Sunday dinner together, and our children could play together and have one another for support as they grew up.'' She turned to Mariah with a sigh. ''Wouldn't that be just perfect?''

Mariah understood that Parker had no clue she was torturing her. So she simply nodded, finding it easy to buy into that dream. It was what she'd imagined when she'd gotten married—families reaching from the past to the future, an ongoing stream of love and support. It was hard to realize that that stopped with her.

A couple of boys ran by, shouting to each other, and Parker seemed to snap back to reality. She blinked at Mariah, as though just realizing what she'd said. ''That didn't hurt you, did it? I mean, even though we're still childless, I want to believe that one day our kids will play together and we'll have those Sunday dinners.''

Mariah smiled. ''I'm sure you can have that, and I'd love to come as long as I can be the eccentric bachelor-girl aunt who brings back presents from exotic places.''

Parker gave her an impatient look. ''That isn't what you want and…'' She raised a hand for silence before Mariah could interrupt with a denial. ''It isn't, and you know it. You're beginning to want Cam. I can see it in your face.''

Oh, God, Mariah thought. Could *he?*

''It may be what I want,'' she admitted in a whisper, making sure no one else could hear, ''but I know I can't have it. He'll want his own children, and I don't want to deprive him of them.''

''Maybe he wants you more.''

Mariah rolled her eyes. ''I don't think so. We barely tolerate each other.''

''Because you can't find a way to deal with the attraction. It's there, but you don't like it when it hurts, so you keep trying to put it away. Love isn't that manageable.''

''Yeah, well, love and attraction are not the same thing.''

''Maybe, but when you're obviously experiencing both, you'd better find a way to deal with your desire for him before it chomps its way out of you like some extraplanetary monster.''

Mariah turned to her sister at that dramatic metaphor, the tension easing. "That's a little theatrical even for you. Each of us will find our way. Just don't try to force on me what you want for yourself. I'll be fine. I've been wanting to go to Europe for so long."

"You're going to be lonely," Parker predicted.

Mariah shook her head. "I'm going to find myself."

Parker growled impatiently. "You're so lost the CIA wouldn't be able to find you."

CHAPTER TEN

ST. ANTHONY'S PARISH HALL, festooned with crepe
paper streamers in blue and gold—the school's colors—was bursting with patrons for the chicken dinner. The laughter and conversation were so loud that
Cam had to put his lips to Mariah's ear to be heard.
He didn't mind that at all.

Earlier, he'd stopped by her booth, intending to
help her and Parker take down their pavilions, only
to find that Gary Warren and his kids were already
there, pulling Parker's apart.

Gary had spotted him, and with a broad smile
held a post in one hand as he reached out with the
other to shake his hand. Cam had moved forward to
help Parker, struggling with a large box of oils and
ointments.

"How'd it go?" he'd asked, taking the box from
her.

"Very well," she'd replied, her cheeks pink, her
eyes alight. "I made a small fortune, and Mariah
sold just about everything she brought with her."

Mariah had looked up from the screen she was
folding. "Okay, how come she has all the help? Is

my abs exercise tape finally working and I look as though I don't need any?''

Gary's kids had hurried to help her. Jeff was a senior at Maple Hill High, and Stacey, a junior. They were redheaded and tall—attributes stocky, dark-haired Gary said they'd acquired from their mother.

Cam had wondered what Gary was doing here, then saw a look pass between him and Parker that made it pretty clear. Romance was in bloom.

''I'll take that to the car for her,'' Gary had offered. Cam had handed it over and watched them walk away, exchanging some private remark that made them laugh.

He'd turned back to the tent and caught Mariah watching them, too, her expression difficult to read. He'd been unable to tell if she approved of the relationship or not.

He still couldn't tell, though they'd all come together to the parish hall. They'd met up with the Lightfoot sisters and the children, and were now part of a line of people waiting to be served that stretched out the door.

Gary and Parker were ahead of them, separated from them by Brian and the twins. Gary's kids had joined their friends, Letitia and Lavinia were sitting at a table with Mr. Groman and the girls were clustered around Cam and Mariah, giggling over some treasure they'd won at the coin toss.

''You don't like him?'' Cam asked Mariah, having to get so close to make himself heard that he felt the fragrant silkiness of her hair against his cheek and his nose.

She turned in surprise. "Who?"

"Gary."

"Yes, I do like him," she corrected. "I just worry about her."

"She seems very capable to me. And isn't she older than you are?"

"Yes. But she's all heart and falls in love very quickly. I don't want her to be disappointed again." She stood on tiptoe to ask him, "Do you know him very well?" Her lips bumped his earlobe and he had to put an arm around her to steady her as the line moved forward. Pretending to remain unaffected took considerable effort.

"As well as co-workers do. I'm not familiar with gardening, but he appears to be very good at it. They've hired him to do summer flower baskets on the square, and to put flowers around the Minuteman and his lady."

She nodded. "His kids seem sweet and well adjusted."

"He does a lot with them. He's always trying to schedule work around their games and activities."

"Good fathers aren't always good husbands, though."

"I'm sure that's true. But Gary appears to be an all-around nice guy." He grinned. "Maybe you'll have to get him alone and interrogate him to find out the truth. You're pretty scary when you want to be.''

He was surprised when she smiled. "That doesn't seem to have put you at a distance."

He shrugged. "If you survive a bad childhood, you grow up fearless. You've already stared into the face of stuff most people never have to deal with."

Their discussion was interrupted suddenly when Mariah, counting noses, realized Brian was missing. "Where did he go?" she asked Peter.

He shrugged. "I don't know. I was at the dessert table."

Mariah stepped out of line to peer down the length of it. There was no sign of the boy. She groaned.

"Maybe he went to the bathroom," Cam suggested. "I'll check."

"I'll look outside." She caught Parker's arm. "Will you and Gary keep an eye on the kids for me? Brian's missing."

Cam dodged the crowd to hurry to the men's room at the far end of the hall. He was instantly rewarded with Brian's reflection in the long mirror over a bank of sinks. The boy washed his hands halfheartedly, then yanked down a wad of paper towels.

"Brian," Cam said, walking into the room. It was lit by the harsh glare of overhead fluorescents and smelled of antiseptic. "Are you all right? We didn't know where you'd gone."

The boy wasn't wearing his usual irrepressible smile. He seemed grim. "I told Pete," he said.

"He was busy checking out the dessert table and didn't hear you. Mariah was afraid something had happened to you."

Brian shook his head. "I'm fine. But the fair's over and that's kind of…you know…the end."

Cam put an arm around his shoulders and led him toward the door. "The end?"

"Of the school year. We're not coming back, you know."

"Yes, I heard that."

Brian stopped in the doorway and gazed up at Cam. "Can we go outside for a minute?"

"Sure. Mariah's out there looking for you."

They stepped out into the twilight. The playground and parking area, which had been so lively just an hour ago, was now bare of the colorful tents and booths. But the stir of conversation remained where people were still putting things away in their cars, calling to one another and laughing.

"I like the trees here," Brian said, looking around him. "At home they're all palms. Some are pretty, but they don't move like these do. Kind of like somebody's dancing."

Cam drew the boy to a bench near the parish hall doorway and sat down. "You'll make friends at another school, Brian," he said, thinking that though the boy's situation was very different, he reminded him of himself. Lots of people moved around in

Brian's life, but no one knew how to change his situation, so he was still isolated and alone. Cam caught the boy's neck in the crook of his arm and pretended to squeeze. "You're a nice kid when you're not making holes in the bathroom wall and falling out of the attic."

Brian grinned reluctantly. "The gold's gotta be in the carriage house somewhere."

"Maybe someone's found it and never told anybody, on the chance he'd have to give it back."

"If it was a kid, he'd be too excited not to tell. And the carriage house has been a kids' dorm since they started using cars instead of horses." He gazed up at Cam and asked seriously, "Do you remember that?"

Cam tightened his elbow. "No, I don't remember that. It had to be eighty years ago. Do I look that old?"

Brian laughed, the sound the first childlike thing Cam had heard out of him since he'd found him.

Cam released him, but his smile lingered. "I'm probably not gonna find it," Brian added, "but I like to think about it. So does Ashley. We're going to spend a whole week going on all the rides at Disneyland."

"Then what?"

"I want to live there, but Ashley says we can't. So we'll go to Disney World in Florida. Then there's a new place in Europe. Mariah said she might go there on her trip." Brian sighed. "If I find the gold,

I'm going with her." He grinned knowingly at Cam. "You'd like to come, too, wouldn't ya? You like her a lot."

"Yes, I do. But she seems to think she'd enjoy the trip more all by herself."

That didn't upset Brian. "Then you and me'll go and we'll just follow her around. Maybe we'll bring Ashley. She's a girl, but she can walk the playground fence without falling off. And she pitches like a guy."

"Sounds like a plan." Cam made himself add, "But you should also have a plan if you *don't* find the gold."

Brian shrugged, looking out into the darkening parking lot. "Then I guess Mariah goes to Europe, you stay here and finish work on the Manor's plumbing and Ashley and I go back to where we always go. At least for the summer. Then we'll have to find new schools."

He sounded accepting of his situation. Cam remembered how awful he'd felt having to accept the unacceptable because there was no way out. He, at least, had had siblings in the same boat. Brian was an only child. Granted, he had more material things than Cam had had, but material things would not have eased his desperate longing for one kind word from either parent.

He gently put a hand to Brian's back. "This is going to sound like a long, long time to you," he said, "but one day you'll look around and realize that you're eighteen, and you can make your own decisions about what you want to do. So make sure you're prepared for when that day comes. Don't learn any bad habits, and be smart so you can take yourself wherever you want to go.''

Brian nodded without enthusiasm. ''Yeah.''

Cam spotted Mariah wandering around the parking lot, scanning the people coming and going. He stood and waved in her direction. ''Mariah!'' he called. ''Over here!''

She ran toward them, the folds of her long cotton skirt moving gracefully around her ankles. ''Is he all right?'' she demanded, leaning over Brian and lifting his chin in her hand. ''Are you okay, sweetie?''

''I'm fine,'' Brian assured her. ''I just went to the bathroom. I told Pete, but I guess he didn't hear me.''

She put a hand to her heart and breathed a sigh of relief. Then she caught Brian's hand and pulled him to his feet. ''Come on, we're missing dinner.''

In a gesture she seemed completely unaware of, she caught Cam's arm and drew him along, too. He told himself to attach no importance to it, and while he accepted that intelligently, his heart couldn't help the cheerful suspicion that he was wearing her down.

IT LOOKED TO MARIAH as though Cam, Gary, Jeff and the children had eaten enough chicken to nullify the intent of the fund-raiser. They all went back several times for more meat, more beans, more corn bread.

Hank, Jackie and their children were seated with the Megraths at the table behind them.

"We're clearing up in a little while for dancing," Hank said to Cam. "We need volunteers."

"I thought the dance was in the gym?" Cam replied.

"That's for the teenagers. This one's for us mature types."

Cam laughed. "Mature? I've seen you push Evan Braga into the lake while on a run rather than let him pass you."

Hank dismissed the incident with a shake of his head. "We had a bet on who could do the fastest lap. There was money at stake. And I meant mature in age. Are you staying to dance?"

Cam turned to Mariah. "Are we staying to dance?"

She searched her brain for an excuse. She'd love to stay and dance with him, and that convinced her that she shouldn't. "I have the children—" she began.

But Hank interrupted. "So does almost everyone here. Some of the teenage girls have set up child care in a couple of the classrooms. We suggest generous tipping, since they're missing the teen dance to do this for us."

Her excuse demolished, Mariah finally nodded.

"Sure." She smiled blandly at Cam. "But *you* have to tip the girls. I'm saving my money to go to Europe, remember?" She wanted to remind him—and herself—that despite the cozy weekend of community effort and tonight's camaraderie, she was moving on.

"How could I forget? You find a way to insert it in every conversation."

"Just want you to bear it in mind."

He nailed her with a glance. Hank and Gary were talking now, and everyone else around them was engaged in other conversations.

"Or maybe you have to keep telling yourself you're planning to go," he said softly, "because you no longer want to leave as badly as you used to."

She was shocked that he'd picked up on her vacillation. She'd done everything she could to pretend it wasn't there.

"Maple Hill was always only a temporary stop for me," she said, her voice less firm than she'd intended. "And my job at the Manor is finished."

"You said Letitia wanted to give you another position."

"It's the ideal time to leave. If I'm going to go, I should go now."

He nodded in amiable agreement. "As long as you're going for the right reasons."

Suddenly, there was a great commotion as Father Chabot stood in the outside doorway and invited the teens to move to the gym, where the band could be heard warming up.

As they streamed out, six girls organized at the other end of the hall and asked that all the children staying for child care gather around them.

Mariah collected her group and took them to the girls as the men began moving tables.

"I didn't know you were staying to dance," Ashley said. "Are you gonna dance with Cam?"

"Probably cheek to cheek," Brian said, catching Julia's hand when she lagged behind. Erica and Rachel Whitcomb followed, each carrying one of their twin brothers. Sister Mary Alice and Sister Theresa from the school were watching infants in the convent.

"No speculating on my love life," Mariah scolded him with a smile. "You guys are all going to be charming and cooperative for the girls, right?"

"Right," they replied in unison.

Mariah turned to Brian, needing extra assurance. "Please, Brian. Promise me you won't look for gold."

He rolled his eyes at her. "I won't. Besides, Debbie Bonatello is one of the girls watching us. Her little brother's in my class. She's a babe. I've wanted to get to know her for a long time."

"Okay, but remember to be polite. I wouldn't call her a babe to her face."

"I know that!"

"Good. That's the sign of a gentleman."

As the girls and the nuns left the room with the children, the atmosphere in the hall changed dramatically. The noise level quieted, tables were folded, and while the men whisked them away to be stored in the basement, the women lined the chairs and benches up along the side of the room. A group of four of Maple Hill's senior citizens, two men and two women who called themselves Golden Oldies, gathered on the stage.

Someone brought them chairs, turned on the stage lights, put a table nearby with a water pitcher and glasses.

The hall lights were dimmed and the Oldies leaned into a circle to tune their instruments. As Hank appeared to wrap his arms around Jackie, and Parker and Gary wandered away, completely unaware of Mariah's presence, Mariah found herself feeling alone. And it wasn't simply the loneliness of solitude, but the loneliness of not being part of a couple.

One moment she was startled, even horrified that she recognized the feeling for what it was, then Cam appeared and she forgot everything except how gorgeous he was in jeans and an Amherst sweatshirt, and how happy she was that he was back.

The music started, a sweet rendition of "Embraceable You," and he opened his arms. She walked into them without hesitation, realizing this as a rare moment that should be enjoyed without too much analysis.

Cam intended to find a topic of conversation that would relax her, help her feel they'd put aside their customary antagonism, but there wasn't time. The instant she walked into his arms he felt her lean into him. There was none of the stiffness he'd expected, no resistance to the intimacy of dancing together. She wrapped her arms around his neck, rested her forehead against his chin and seemed to dissolve into his embrace.

He couldn't think, simply gave himself over to the romantic Gershwin music, the unexpected pleasure of the moment, and danced away with her.

He recognized the evening as a turning point. Up to now, he'd been attracted to Mariah, challenged by her, intrigued, even excited by her physically and emotionally. He'd thought he *might* be falling in love.

Tonight, he knew it with a certainty that changed his perception of everything. As she relaxed in his arms for reasons known only to her, he realized with the sudden brightness of an epiphany that she *was* his.

All he had to do now was make sure she understood that he was hers.

Throughout the evening, their friends changed partners, changed back again, sat on the sidelines to talk, then danced once more. But Cam and Mariah remained wrapped in each other's arms in a small shadowy corner of the floor, moving slowly to the nostalgic tunes the Golden Oldies preferred, not noticing when they played the occasional up-tempo number.

Cam saw things in Mariah's eyes he hadn't seen before. He saw her as she could be with her defenses lowered, sweet and trusting and open.

She made him feel refreshed and renewed, as though this second chance at his life in Maple Hill might really be a new lease on happiness.

Just after ten, she drew away from him with obvious regret. "I have to get the children home," she said, her hands still linked with his.

He felt sixteen. He felt ageless.

Parting from her was the last thing he wanted, but he understood her responsibilities. He was about to tell her he'd take her and the children home, when Letitia appeared beside them.

"You two keep dancing," she said, waving plump hands at them. "Vinnie and I are going to take the children to the dorm and stay so you can enjoy your evening."

Mariah tried to protest. "But you've watched them all weekend. I can't..."

"And you've watched them day and night for months." Letitia patted her cheek. "Don't hurry home. We don't intend to wait up. You two have a wonderful time, stay up to watch the sunrise, whatever you want to do. Don't worry about the kids." Then she walked away.

"I feel so guilty," Mariah said to Cam.

He leaned down and kissed her soundly. "Don't

waste time on that. She wants you to enjoy yourself. Come on.'' He swirled her away, then was forced to stop abruptly when the music changed to a rumba.

Everyone on the dance floor looked at everyone else, the style uncharacteristic for the Golden Oldies. But Gary and Parker were getting into it, and Hank and Jackie made a brave attempt. Haley, apparently feeling too pregnant to try, led Bart off the floor.

"Can you rumba?" Mariah asked Cam with a grin.

"No," he replied honestly, noting the spark of laughter in her eyes and thinking this night was indeed a miracle. "Can you?"

She nodded. "I dated a boy from Cuba in college. It's simple. It's just a matter of step, close, step." She demonstrated. "Shifting your weight and moving your hips."

She demonstrated again, putting her hips into it this time as she turned. She held her arms out, feet and hands keeping the rhythm, her hips in the simple cotton skirt taking him to the edge of apoplexy.

She caught his hands, encouraging him to move with her. He had to struggle to concentrate.

The number was over before they were able to move in sync and she collapsed against him laughing when the Oldies picked up with a romantic rendition of "Cape Cod Bay."

"We'll have to work on that," she said, sounding a little breathless. "I'd forgotten how much fun the rumba can be. Or just how much fun dancing can be.''

He had to agree. "I haven't had the opportunity to do that much since high school. Most of the functions my wife and I attended were more formal and serious.''

Mariah nodded. "We did lots of things with Ben's family. They were very nice, but there were so many of them there wasn't time or room in our lives for friends. I think that's why he wanted his own children so desperately. He must have felt like a failure in his big family.''

The thought seemed to eclipse her mood.

"Let's not talk about our exes," he said, hating to lose the wonder of this night. "Did I tell you I'm buying Hank's house on the lake?''

"No." She looked at him with interest. "Don't he and Jackie live near downtown?''

"They do. That's Jackie's place. In his bachelor days, Hank bought a great place on the far side of the lake. But the house in town works better for Jackie's job as mayor and for the children, so he's selling it to me and they're going to find something a little farther away for a weekend and holiday getaway. You have to come and see it. He's already given me the key, but we don't sign papers for a few more days, so I hate to go in until it's mine.''

"Fred will like that," she predicted with a smile.

"I'm sure he will. It's a great place for children and pets.''

She didn't tune out when he mentioned children. "Do you fish?" she asked.

"Not successfully, no. But I plan to improve my technique after I move in. I just bought a four-man rowboat from Jimmy Elliott."

"Just sunbathing on a boat would be nice."

"Then I'll have to get something in the yacht class. That might take a while. But you can sunbathe on the deck of the house."

He saw reality struggle to take control in her eyes. She sighed, possibly trying to fend it off. "Are you going to have a housewarming when you're finally in?"

"Good idea," he praised. "You can help me. Your children should all be on their way home by then."

She looked cautious and opened her mouth to reply, but he forestalled her with "Don't tell me you'll be on your way to Europe. I'm working on a fantasy here."

She smiled—the curve of her lips both sweet and sad. "Okay. We'll say I'll help you. I presume you're talking cooking and not housecleaning."

"Right. We've got someone at Whitcomb's who's already agreed to clean for me in exchange for the occasional barbecue."

"Now, there's an arrangement. Can I work the same bargain?"

He kissed her. "It's a deal."

"Aren't we supposed to seal it with a handshake?" she asked, laughing.

His hands rested lightly in the middle of her back and he pressed gently. He wouldn't have moved hers, wrapped around his neck, for all the gold in the treasury. "Not when our hands are otherwise occupied."

She looked into his eyes, the expression in hers changing from levity to seriousness without warning, then she tightened her grip on him, leaned her head against him and fell silent.

He held her tightly, feeling the night slip away from him and willing to do anything to hold on to it.

CHAPTER ELEVEN

THE GOLDEN OLDIES PLAYED "Good Night, Sweet-heart" at 2:00 a.m. Cam and Mariah, the Megraths, the Whitcombs and Parker and Gary met at the sparsely occupied Breakfast Barn for coffee. Two young busboys pulled a couple of tables together and the group settled in, high on friendship and good cheer.

"I haven't been up this late on noncity business," Jackie said, "since before Rachel was born."

"Me, either." Gary seated Parker, then sat beside her. "The last time I was up after midnight was New Year's Eve, 1995. I remember because Jeff, who was nine at the time, had climbed onto the roof to blow my old bosun's pipe, fell off and broke his leg and mine."

While everyone else sympathized, Jackie laughed. "Kids do make dates memorable. I remember my thirtieth birthday because my girls gave me chicken pox."

A waitress appeared amid the laughter and groans and they were forced to concentrate on their menus instead of the conversation. But the moment she left it began again.

Mariah listened quietly to one story after another of how children made even usually ordinary occasions momentous. She glanced at Bart to see if he was affected by the reminiscences. She knew he'd lost his unborn twins when his first wife had died.

But he was laughing, his pregnant wife apparently blunting the pain and loss of the past. Even Haley had a story about the baby giving her morning sickness when she interviewed the governor of the state, who was visiting Maple Hill.

Parker seemed to find Gary's stories endlessly amusing. His children appeared to like her, and she claimed to like them. If this relationship between Parker and Gary worked out, the children wouldn't be a problem.

Cam, too, laughed at their stories.

That was a good thing, she thought, as she regained emotional equilibrium after her fantasy evening. She'd indulged herself with the pretense that she and Cam had nothing to worry about but each other, and she'd found it delicious. Now she had to remember the truth.

She couldn't have children. She wasn't whining or engaging in self-pity; she was simply reminding herself of the very real barrier to Cam's happiness—and her own.

Should she develop a serious relationship with Cam and they got married, he would be odd man out on every occasion like this. Every time men pulled their wallets out to show off photos of children stamped with their features, he'd have to simply watch and listen rather than participate. Whenever parents talked about the fearless boy who took after his father, or the girl who wanted to be president because she was just like her brilliant mother, he would have to sit back quietly.

That had been so clear to her when Ben had left, but in her loneliness recently, she'd forgotten how that inability to reproduce struck at the heart of a man. It had once struck at her own heart, but she'd adjusted. It was harder for a man, though. He thought of himself as the link between past and future, and if he loved *her,* the chain would be broken.

Though she kept an outward appearance of cheer for the sake of their companions, she felt sadness settle inside her like a cold brick.

When they finally all said goodbye at 3:30 a.m., Cam took her back to the school parking lot to pick up her car. The place was dark and deserted now, with not even the sound of insects on the air. Everything was asleep.

He walked around his truck to open her door. She rose out of the vehicle and into his arms as naturally as if they were on their honeymoon. He felt the urgency in her as she clung to him.

"Don't go to the Manor," he whispered, kissing her cheek, her eyes, her lips. "Come home with me.

I'll bring you back in time to get the kids ready for school. I promise.''

She returned his kisses, held him one extra moment, then dropped her arms, her voice calm but firm. "I can't," she said. Then she looked into his eyes, her own filled with an unsettling resolve. "Cameron, you have to understand me when I tell you this isn't going to work. I'm going to be gone, and the best thing you can do for yourself is find someone who can be everything you need."

He knew this speech. He'd heard it several times in one form or another since the night he'd rescued her from Brian's flood.

It exasperated him, and it terrified him. He wanted to shake her for presuming to think she knew what he wanted, and he wished there were some way to make it clear to her that his future would be even colder than his past if she wasn't in it.

But she might already know that. That was probably why she insisted on pushing him away. She knew that what they shared was significant, and she didn't want to take the chance that it might hurt her.

"I don't need you to be anything for me except what you need to be for yourself." He realized there was little point in arguing with her, but he'd be damned if he'd let her blame him for this. "Maybe a little braver—a little more daring."

Tears welled in her eyes. "Do you have any idea how much courage it takes to get pregnant when you know there's a fifty-fifty chance the baby won't survive—again? And to somehow know you're always on the wrong side of the gamble?''

He regretted his remark immediately, and put a hand to her arm and rubbed gently. ''I'm sorry. I'm not minimizing what you've been through. I'm just trying to make you understand that while it was traumatic for Ben, I don't care. Let's get married and adopt a whole passel of children if you want to. Your life isn't over because you can't give birth.''

Her lips firmed. ''I am not going to argue this with you again,'' she said. ''My life is my business.''

''Pardon me,'' he corrected her calmly, ''but when it's tied to mine, 'your business' is a partnership. We *are* going to argue this.''

In the yard of the residence behind the school, a dog barked loudly. Across the street, another dog barked in reply.

''You're waking up the neighborhood!'' she whispered harshly, trying to push him back toward his truck.

Intrepidly, he followed her to her car. ''If you'd accepted my invitation,'' he reminded her quietly, ''we'd be on our way to my place by now and we wouldn't be bothering anybody—except each other.''

She stopped at her car door to jab his chest with her index finger. ''Sex doesn't solve everything! You think you'll show me how wonderful it is to make love with you and I'll abandon my dreams of Europe so you can have what you want?''

He slapped her hand away and glowered down at her, now annoyed. ''No. I thought I'd show you how wonderful it is for us to make love, and give you back your dreams of home and family. We can have that. You're just afraid of it!''

His voice had risen despite his efforts to keep it down, and the dogs now barked continuously.

''I'm afraid,'' she said, enunciating, her eyes sparking in the dark, ''that if I stay here a moment longer I'm going to slug you!''

He took a step back and spread his arms. ''Hey,'' he challenged. ''Give me your best shot. I'm more than ready.''

For an exciting instant, he thought she was going to take him up on the offer. Instead, she ripped open her door, got in her car and turned on the motor.

From the yard next door, someone shouted, ''Go home and fight, for God's sake!''

She backed out of her parking spot with a squeal of brakes and roared away, thinking, he guessed, that she'd won the argument.

She had a thing or two to learn about him.

MARIAH HAD NO IDEA what to do about Cam. It had been four days since their argument, and while she hadn't seen him, not gotten a call from him in that time, he'd done other, more insidious, things to completely distract her and—frankly—charm her. And she didn't want to be charmed. She didn't.

But the morning after their argument, she left the house with the children for the walk to school and there'd been a French bouquet spilling gloriously out of the mailbox. A tag with her name was attached and nothing else.

The following day she'd awakened to a mild thumping on her bedroom window. She'd turned groggily to find colorful orbs bumping against it. She'd sat up abruptly, rubbing her eyes, wondering what on earth they were.

A closer investigation revealed a bouquet of balloons tied to the temperature gauge outside her bedroom window—on the second floor!

A single red Mylar balloon in the shape of a heart bore her name.

The day after, when she'd arrived home from an errand on which Letitia had sent her, she found the kitchen table set for two with china, crystal and flowers. A white-jacketed waiter with a black bow tie served her a crab-and-shrimp Caesar salad with cheese bread and an iced mocha. That was her favorite meal at the Old Post Road Inn, where she and Parker sometimes met for lunch. She suspected collusion.

Taped to the chair pulled up to the second place setting was a note that read: ''Imagine I'm here, then think about how much more fun this meal would be if you didn't have to imagine it.''

"Arrogant!" she muttered.

"No, ma'am," the waiter countered as he offered her more cheese bread. "Honest."

On this, the fourth morning, Mariah was almost afraid to get out of bed. But the children were already collected in her doorway, enjoying her mysterious surprises as much as she was confounded by them. They knew as well as she did that Cam was at the bottom of the mysteries.

"There's nothing downstairs!" Brain reported.

"And nothing in the mailbox!" Ashley added. All the children ran to her window.

"And nothing on the thermometer!" Jessica said. "Maybe there's no surprise today."

"There has to be a surprise," Ashley said. "There's been one every day."

"Maybe Cam gave up," Brian suggested.

Ashley shook her head. "He'd never give up. You don't get to be successful if you give up. The Gypsy prince told me."

Brian rolled his eyes. "That was make-believe."

"Make-believe," she explained didactically, "can come true. I'm going to be a ballerina."

"Okay, okay." Mariah raised both hands to stop the argument. "If you'll all get breakfast on the table while I shower and dress, I'll take you out to the Barn tonight for dinner to celebrate tomorrow being the last day of school."

The twins and the Morris girls left her room in a gale of laughter and cheers. Ashley and Brian, how-

ever, looked at each other, their response to the end
of school understandably less enthusiastic.

They finally followed the others, Ashley saying
hopefully to Brian, "Maybe you'll find the money
today."

Mariah fell back to the mattress with a groan.
She'd have to remember to wear her boots and a
hard hat if Brian was going to keep looking.

Breakfast was uneventful. She walked the children to school, checked the mailbox on her way
back and found a Priority Mail package from the
travel agent with whom she'd made arrangements
for her trip. She ripped open the envelope to discover her tickets, an itinerary and several brochures
she'd requested. She left in six days.

She stood there with everything she'd wanted this
entire year spread out in the palms of her hands. Her
pulse quickened; her hands shook just a little. At
last. Escape.

She froze, wondering why she'd chosen that
word. Escape? Why would she sum up the dream of
a lifetime in a word that suggested bailing out? Because that wasn't what she was doing.

Okay, the trip wasn't the dream of a lifetime; it
was a fairly recent passion. She'd always loved her
art but had never believed she could pursue it before
until…until she had nothing else to do.

But it was a noble goal. She was going to Europe
to learn, to improve herself, to make a life that

would be fulfilling now that husband and family were out of the question.

She was still analyzing when she heard the unmistakable note of a pitch pipe. She looked up to discover six young people ranged in a row, blocking the carriage house's front door. They were a mixed group of teens, boys and girls, and they were dressed in black pants, white shirts, red vests and straw hats. She recognized Gary Warren's children and Mike McGee, the young man Haley and Bart had taken under their wing.

She took all this in with a sense of disbelief. Had she stepped back in time to the movie set of *Meet Me in St. Louis?*

The group burst into song. With a sort of barbershop harmony in keeping with their costumes, they sang about two people being meant for each other, about how heaven must have sent one to the other, gathering all the qualities one had longed for and rolling them into one perfect package.

Mariah stared. After the first verse, they broke into a Busby Berkeley sort of tap dance, with broad smiles and big movements.

That finished, they sang another verse, then finished on a high note, arms extended to the sky. Then Stacey Warren came forward, handed Mariah a note that said they were the Maple Hill High School Madrigals and were available for weddings, parties and dances, and that the proceeds from their work would take them to the All Schools Competition in New York in January.

She gave Mariah a giant chocolate kiss wrapped in red cellophane with a silver bow and said perkily, "Our performance was compliments of Mr. Cameron Trent."

Mariah didn't know how to explain that she was shocked but not surprised. That wouldn't have made sense. But, then, nothing about Cam's insistence that they have a relationship did.

"Thank you," she said. "I enjoyed it very much."

The girl grinned. "Thank you. Please tell your friends about us. We have to make a small fortune by the holidays."

"I certainly will."

Stacey hurried off to the van all the others were piling into. Parked beside it was Cam's truck, Cam himself leaning against the front fender. When the van drove off, he walked across the lawn toward Mariah, Fred barking from the truck. She had to remember that his charming attitude today would not survive his eventual disappointment in her. He didn't realize it, but it wouldn't. She'd seen Ben change from the man who'd loved her to the man who resented her. She had to make Cam understand once and for all that what he wanted was not going to happen.

"They're pretty good, aren't they?" he asked, taking her mail from her as she fiddled with her key.

She gave him a glare over her shoulder, pushed the door open, yanked him inside with her, then pushed the door closed and confronted him with both hands on her hips.

"Cameron Trent," she said firmly, looking him right in the eye. "I don't love you. If I can make it any plainer, please tell me how. I am not going out with you again. We are not going to have a relationship. *It's over.* Do you hear me? Over!"

He shifted his weight and folded his arms, her mail caught against his chest. "Then you're admitting that it *was.*"

"I'm not admitting anything except that you're starting to annoy me beyond reason! Look!"

She snatched the mail from him, tossed everything but the package from the travel agent at a chair and waved the ticket in front of him. "I'm leaving next Wednesday and you will never see me again! Is that clear? I do not want to marry you, or love you, or whatever it is you want from me."

He caught her wrist and pulled it down so that he could see her face above the tickets. "But you do," he said, "love me. You may not want to, but you do."

She turned away on the pretense of gathering up the mail so he wouldn't see that that was true. "Cam, this is bordering on harassment. Go away!"

The sudden peal of the doorbell was a surprising sound in the middle of their argument. Cam, still standing just inside the door, reached an arm out and opened it.

Letitia stood there, her face pale. She looked at Mariah in relief, then at Cam in surprise. "Thank goodness you're here, too."

Mariah braced herself for bad news. "What is it?"

"Ashley's guardian passed away during the night." She looked from one to the other again. "I spoke to him on the phone just two days ago, and he expected to live until the holidays. He said he and Ashley had a long talk on the phone Sunday night and he'd promised to take her to see the Joffrey Ballet."

Mariah felt her heart lurch. Poor Ashley. Who would decide her future now? She prayed that Walter Kerwin had made sound arrangements for her. Tears burned her eyes and emotion clogged her throat. Ashley was such a game little girl, always trying to adjust, always eager to please. She dreaded having to tell her.

"Do you want me to get her out of class?" Mariah asked.

Letitia shook her head. "She's already in my office with Lavinia and Mr. Beresford."

"Mr. Beresford?"

"Mr. Kerwin's lawyer. He's here to…to conduct some business."

"Ashley business?"

Letitia waved her hands in the air. "It's complicated and a little…tricky. Come with me to my office.'' She caught Cam's arm and leaned on him. ''You, too.''

''But I don't know anything about Ashley's guardian,'' he said.

She nodded. ''He seems to have known something about you.''

He turned a questioning eye on Mariah, who shrugged and followed them out the door.

Lavinia, Ashley and Noel Beresford, a tall, youngish man with dark hair and a designer suit, had pulled their chairs into a circle.

As Mariah, Letitia and Cam walked in, the lawyer stood and Lavinia excused herself to get more chairs. Cam went to help her.

The ''tricky'' business they were conducting did not seem to be going well. Lavinia looked wide-eyed with concern, and Ashley was pale, her expression forlorn. She ran to Mariah, and though she wasn't crying, her slender frame was trembling.

No surprise there, Mariah thought. Every child had a basic right to family and a sense of security—two things this child was continually deprived of. Mariah wrapped her arms around her and drew her back to the chair she'd occupied, sharing it with her.

''Honey, I'm so sorry,'' Mariah whispered. ''But I'm sure Mr. Kerwin made good plans for you.''

Ashley apparently found no comfort in that. She sat with her arms folded, staring at the Oriental carpet.

Three chairs from the library were fitted into the circle; Noel Beresford resumed his place and smiled. He appeared affable, Mariah noted, and not at all affected by whatever had upset the Lightfoot sisters and Ashley. Lawyers, she imagined, had to maintain a certain distance from their clients' problems.

Letitia made halfhearted introductions, no doubt eager to get down to business. "Mr. Beresford, Mariah and Cameron. Children, this is Mr. Beresford, Walter Kerwin's attorney."

He smiled around the circle. "So. You've explained why I'm here, Miss Lightfoot?"

Letitia frowned. "No," she said on a hesitant note, then added more firmly, "No. I thought it would be best coming from you."

"Well." He opened a file folder in his lap and squared up the papers inside on his knee. "I guess the best thing to do is come straight to the point." He smiled at Mariah, then, curiously, at Cam and said, "I imagine you'll both have questions afterward, but I'm sure I can answer all those. Let me just tell you that Walter has mentioned the two of you in his will. I'll read you the pertinent passages."

Mariah would have questioned that she rated a mention in Walter Kerwin's will, but she saw Cam, clearly as puzzled as she was, simply lean back and give the man his full attention. She decided that was a good idea. With an arm around Ashley, who continued to tremble, she listened.

Noel Beresford looked up from his notes to smile

again. "He left a considerable endowment to the school, then he mentions the two of you. Now, where...oh, yes. Here it is." He cleared his throat:

And to Cameron and Mariah Trent I leave custody of my ward, Ashley Weisfield. Having been aware of my condition for some time, I studied friends and acquaintances, searching for a good situation for Ashley, one that would provide her with the siblings and playmates I've been unable to supply. But most of my friends are of my own age, and therefore unsuitable. I did not want to leave her in the care of a guardian again, as I've realized over time how sadly I've failed her as a parent and would not wish to impose such a situation on her again.

So I went to the source. In a lengthy conversation with Ashley, which I have recorded, I asked her if she had her choice of the perfect family, with whom she would like to live. She answered without hesitation—"With Mr. and Mrs. Trent."

Beresford looked up to smile at them again, and continued.

I include this in my will now because of the unpredictability of the course of my illness, and will follow this up with a discussion with Mr. and Mrs. Trent.

Beresford lowered the sheet of paper, his expression now grave. "Unfortunately, he passed away before he had the opportunity to do so. So, Mr. and Mrs. Trent, I'm sure this comes as quite a surprise, but I also see that you seem very fond of Ashley and hope you can accommodate Mr. Kerwin's wishes."

Mariah couldn't think, couldn't imagine, how this mistake had been made. She opened her mouth to speak, but didn't know what to say. She didn't want to betray Ashley by telling Beresford that she and Cam weren't husband and wife, weren't even engaged, weren't even intending…well, *he* might be, but she wasn't!

Cam hadn't said anything, either. She glanced at him and saw that he was watching her, apparently preparing to follow her lead.

Mariah was desperately trying to decide on a course of action, when Ashley burst into tears. "I'm sorry!" she sobbed. "I'm sorry! I shouldn't have lied! But he asked if I could have anything I wanted, and…he never said that before. He always just told me where I had to go. And it was my chance. The Gypsy said so!"

Beresford, now not only puzzled but alarmed, asked with a wince, "The Gypsy?"

Ashley nodded. "He told my fortune at the fair. He said I had to make my own happiness! That I had to decide what I wanted and be responsible for getting it. So I did. I wanted to live with Mariah and Cam, so that's what I told Mr. Kerwin!''

She collapsed against Mariah, crying her heart out.

Beresford looked from Mariah to Cam. "You mean...you're not married?''

Mariah turned to Letitia, who'd also apparently kept that secret, probably unsure how Mariah and Cam would react and, in Ashley's interest, unwilling to betray them.

"No, we're not," Mariah said. Then she, who had never been a mother but always thought like one, instantly abandoned her plan of solitary travel and asked urgently, "Couldn't you just give her to me?" She looked down at Ashley, but the child was still pressed against her, weeping. "We get along well, I've taken care of her for—''

Beresford was shaking his head. "The will says Mr. and Mrs. Cameron Trent. If we do anything other than what's specified in the will, Children and Family Services will have to be informed. There'll be interviews, home studies, possibly other homes considered.''

Hating that she had to do this but realizing that getting a well-meaning but beleaguered agency involved would mean bureaucracy and red tape, Mariah turned to Cam. Certainly he understood Ashley's desperate situation.

CAM READ THE LOOK in Mariah's eyes and knew that fate was handing him a golden opportunity.

Self-preservation skills honed on years of rejection and neglect rose to point him in the direction that would serve his needs.

"Mr. Beresford," he said, leaning forward in his chair, "would you excuse Mariah and me for a few minutes, please?"

Letitia sprang out of her chair as though ejected. "Use the office. Vinnie and I will take Mr. Beresford for a cup of tea. Mr. Beresford, you'd like that, wouldn't you?"

Before the lawyer could express concern over the turn of events, Lavinia whisked him out into the hallway, while Letitia lingered to blow them a kiss, then caught Ashley's hand and followed her sister. Cam smiled to himself. Collaborators on all sides.

He had to play this cool.

The moment the door closed behind Letitia, Mariah stood in agitation and paced back and forth from the chair to the window, finally leaning against the front of Letty's desk.

"You're going to make me ask you, aren't you?" She met his gaze cautiously, aware her cause was too desperate for her to risk being belligerent.

He had to make this hard for her; otherwise, if things didn't have the positive outcome he hoped for, she might blame him down the road for the fact that she'd had to marry him after all. He wanted her to feel responsible for what they had to do.

"I don't know what to say, Mariah." He stretched

out his legs and crossed them at the ankles. "Just fifteen minutes ago you were telling me you never wanted to see me again. You even threatened to have me arrested."

"Fifteen minutes ago," she reminded him, "we didn't know Walter Kerwin had died." She came toward him, her eyes sparking, her manner suggesting she was forgetting her underdog position. "And who told Ashley to take charge of her own destiny?" she demanded. "Huh? Who, O Mighty Stick-in-the-Works son of Othar?"

He returned her glare intrepidly. "That was good advice and you know it." He grinned. "Who expected her to follow through on it with such... style?"

Apparently unable to dispute that, Mariah turned away from him and went back to the desk; she sank onto the end of it with both hands to her face.

"What'll it take?" she finally asked quietly.

"For what?" he asked, pretending innocence. He couldn't say he was precisely enjoying this, but he did appreciate having the advantage for a change.

She huffed a long-suffering sigh and replied without looking at him, "For you to marry me. Something short-term. Something that'll allow us to get her, then when it's all legal, file for divorce so she can come with me. What'll it take?"

"Well," he answered, "a clarification of terms, for one thing."

She straightened off the desk, her expression cautious but hopeful. "What terms? What do you mean?"

"Tell me what you have in mind exactly," he said. "Then I'll tell you whether or not I agree with it."

She paced across the office and back. She was buying time, and he could understand that. This had all happened so quickly, so unexpectedly, that she was making things up as she went along.

"Okay." She stopped pacing finally and took the chair next to his. She sat sideways in it, both hands on the arm of his chair. He could feel her energy, her need for his cooperation. He forced himself to remain relaxed. "I *don't* want to be married."

He nodded once. "So you've made clear."

"But Ashley needs us."

"I agree."

"If we marry, we can claim her."

"Yes."

"But I don't want to stay married."

"Poor example to set for a child."

She growled impatiently. "It'll get her what she wants. She'll understand."

"She wants both of us, if you'll recall," he pointed out calmly.

She sighed. "Do you want to help her or not?"

"I'm listening." Though he knew he wasn't going to get terms he could be happy with, she might come up with something he could settle for in hope of better times.

"Two months," she said abruptly. "A marriage without sex, then I obtain a divorce and take her with me to Europe."

"No," he said.

She uttered a gasp of indignation. "No to what?"

"No to all of it," he replied. "Two months isn't long enough for her to get her bearings. I am not agreeing to a marriage without lovemaking, and I thought you were going to Europe to find yourself? You can't just haul her out of school and drag her around with you while you search for a meaning to your life."

"I can home-school her while we're touring. That's a very acceptable way for a child to be educated today. There are well-outlined programs. And what she'll see in Europe will contribute to, not detract from, her education."

He had to give her that. "But what about you?"

"I'm thinking of her."

Hmm. That was interesting, and possibly a step in his favor. "Okay. Maybe Europe wouldn't hurt her. But two months together isn't long enough."

She folded her arms and faced him, sitting up stiffly. "How long do you want?"

"At least a year," he said.

"A year is too long."

"A year."

"You're being obstructive."

He smiled blandly. "I'm not surprised you recognize the tactic."

She sighed. "All right. A year."

"And we work at being married. Otherwise we aren't giving Ashley what she wants."

She said with disdain, "I suppose by that you mean we have sex."

"By that I mean," he corrected her, sitting up, drawing his legs in, "that we behave with each other as though we want to get along and create a home for this child."

She looked momentarily chastened. He added with more than a little enjoyment, "And we make love as regularly as we're inclined."

"I won't be inclined."

"You're wrong about that."

"I won't."

"When you are," he insisted, "you just have to say so."

She tried to stare him down on that point, but he didn't blink. She finally dropped her lashes, then told him with sudden briskness, "Then we're agreed. We get married for a year, make love when we're so inclined—" her tone clearly added, *Like that'll happen* "—and after a year we divorce, I get custody and take her to Europe."

The terms were bad, but they would give him his chance, and he was sure that was all he needed.

"And, of course," she added, "we make Beresford believe we've been planning to marry all along and we're eager to do this or he might decide this does not comply with his client's wishes at all.''

She offered her hand.

He took it. "Agreed," he said.

CHAPTER TWELVE

THE OFFICE WAS CHAOS when the meeting reconvened and Cam and Mariah shared their decision.

"And when will you do this?" Beresford asked.

Mariah opened her mouth to say that it would take a little time for blood tests, to get a plan together, to...

"This weekend," Cam said.

The lawyer appeared pleased. "Good. I'll stay for the wedding and while I'm here I can get the information I need from you to file adoption proceedings." He drew a deep breath as he looked out the window at the tops of spring-green maple trees. "One could get addicted to this place."

"This weekend!" Letitia said, walking halfway to the door, then turning back. "There's so much to prepare! Do you have a preference of churches? And where should we have the reception?"

Lavinia said, her eyes wide, "The Franklins, Mrs. Morris and Brian's mother will be arriving tomorrow to take the children home. We mustn't forget that in all the excitement. Oh, dear. And you'll need things. Flowers and a photographer and someone to sing 'Oh, Promise Me'—oof!''

Letitia and Lavinia collided in a dramatic meeting of considerable bosoms.

"We'll take care of everything," Cam said. "You ladies don't have to fuss."

"Nonsense!" Letitia was firm. "Mariah's very dear to us, and you, Cameron, have bailed us out of so many plumbing crises that you've become dear to us, too. And since neither of you has parents, we're taking over. I'm sure Parker will understand and want to help us. Or want us to help her."

The group disbanded shortly after, but Ashley hung back in the hallway, her face still pale, confusion in her eyes.

Mariah put a hand to her face. "What is it, Ashley?"

"I don't understand what happened," the child admitted. She peered around Mariah at Cam, who'd been headed for the stairs and had turned back when he realized they'd stopped. "Miss Lightfoot was talking about a church and a reception."

Mariah nodded. "Because we're getting married."

Ashley met her eyes, as though waiting for more.

"So we can adopt you," Cam added.

Ashley glanced from one to the other, a tear sliding down her cheek. "And we're going to...live together?"

"Yes," Mariah confirmed.

"In a house I just bought on the lake," Cam explained. "The three of us and Fred."

"Isn't that what you want?" Mariah asked when the child continued to appear uncertain.

"Yes!" Ashley confirmed quickly. "It's just that...I never really get what I want. So I was just...wondering if I had it right."

"You have it right." Mariah hugged her. "Now, would you like to go back to the dorm and rest? You can have the day off."

Ashley shook her head. "I feel sad about Mr. Kerwin, but..." She smiled for the first time since the strange meeting had begun. She came to Cam, wrapped her arms around his middle and held on.

He kissed the top of her head, determined to give her what she wanted—permanently.

"I want to go back to class," she said, "and tell everybody!"

She ran down the stairs with a squeal of delight, leaving Cam and Mariah to stare at each other in the hallway.

"This is all your fault, you know," she said, marching past him on the stairs.

"My *fault?*" he asked, following her. "I thought it was all *thanks* to me."

"We're tricking her," she said, pushing her way through the big double doors to the sunny morning outside.

"We're rescuing her from a life of loneliness," he corrected her. He caught Mariah's arm and yanked her to a stop. "And who proposed to whom, Miss Mercer?"

"All right, all right!" She shook off his arm and glared at him. "Now we have a little girl thinking she has a family for a lifetime when that isn't true."

"The deal," he reminded her in a stern tone, "was that we put everything into the marriage while we're together."

Her shoulders sagged, as though she knew she couldn't blame him but was having second thoughts about her solution. "We're not going to mar her forever, are we?"

"No," he replied.

She expelled a breath and seemed to acquire new resolve.

"Fine. Well, I have a lot to do." She started off again down the path toward the carriage house.

Again he followed. Fred barked at him as he approached the truck, the dog's head sticking out of the open window. "I'll come by in the morning, and we can move some of your things over."

"Can you make it afternoon?" she asked over her shoulder. "Parents will be picking up their children in the morning and I'd like to be there. All the kids are supposed to be gone by noon."

"Of course. In the afternoon, then."

Weird day, he thought as he climbed into his truck, Fred kissing his ear. He'd begun the morning by having Mariah serenaded with a romantic tune, in the hope of scaling the battlements she'd erected between them. Now, at just—he glanced at his watch; could it be only 11:00 a.m.?—he was scheduled to marry her in four short days. And the battlements remained.

Should make for an interesting marriage.

MARIAH CANCELED HER travel plans. The agent refunded her money, promised to keep her destinations on file and re-create the package if and when Mariah was ready.

She had her belongings packed in an hour, but instead of putting them into storage with what she'd brought with her after her divorce, she put them in a corner of the downstairs hall in preparation for tomorrow's move.

She tried to call Parker, knowing she was at her office in city hall, but her sister didn't pick up.

Mariah spent the rest of the afternoon making sure the children had all their things together—searching under beds, behind drawers and in the bottom of closets for treasures that might have escaped.

Escaped. The word brought to mind her canceled trip. But she had not been escaping, she comforted herself. She'd intended to live a dream.

Instead, she was probably now in for a lot of sleepless nights as she tried to figure out how to cope with Cameron Trent.

But she'd saved Ashley from foster care, and was giving her what she wanted and thought she'd never have.

In all fairness, Mariah had to admit that Cam had helped considerably, though he probably had his own goals in mind. How many men, she wondered, would have risen to an unorthodox proposal quickly enough to save a child from the system? Not many, she was sure. She had to remember that and do her best to comply with his terms. Even if she was never inclined to...

God! How did she get into this mess?

When the children came home, they carried with them armloads of artwork and crafts that they'd made in the classroom. She gave them each a large manila envelope for the flat things, and found some boxes left over from her sign venture for storing their three-dimensional creations.

As they worked, they talked excitedly about her impending marriage to Cam and Ashley's adoption. Amy compared it with a story they'd read in her class. "You might even find out you're a princess!" she said to Ashley.

Jalisa, wide-eyed, suggested she might be able to wear a crown and a frilly gown.

Ashley laughed that off. "No, I won't, but I'll be able to go fishing with Cam in his boat."

The boys seemed to think that was as good as getting to wear a crown. The Morris girls clearly thought she was crazy.

Once all the boxes of belongings were labeled, the children lined them up in the hallway for the morning. A moment of quiet followed as the children realized, probably for the first time, the finality of this move. They had become like a family, but in all probability they would not see one another again.

Before their mood could become maudlin, Mariah packed them all in her van and headed for the Breakfast Barn as she'd promised. They had burgers and fries, and pie for dessert, then she gave each of them a binder she'd prepared with one another's addresses and birth dates, so that they could keep in touch. She'd included photos of special events, as well as the name sign on their bedroom doors.

When they got back to the carriage house, she put in a movie, but they were too restless to watch it. They seemed to want to share fears on their last night together.

The Morris girls were still concerned about their mother's boyfriend.

"Your mom's a smart woman," Mariah reminded them. "And she loves you all very much. She'd never marry someone who'd be mean to you, or whom she thought you wouldn't like. So, give him a chance."

Peter and Philip had just learned that their parents were abandoning stunt work and moving to New York, where their mother had been cast in a small role on Broadway.

"There's gangs and weird people there," Peter said.

Philip agreed with a loud "Yeah!"

"There are also lots of wonderful things to see, and great people doing all kinds of important work. You'll have new opportunities. And your parents will be home more."

"Dad says we'll be able to go to school and live at home." Philip nudged Peter with his elbow. "That'll be cool."

Peter was the adventurer and Philip the homebody. The quiet twin who never did anything but back up his brother, Mariah realized with a private smile, might finally be coming into his own.

Brian had wandered into the kitchen and was sitting on the counter, his head tipped back against the cupboard as he stared upward. He'd been morose all evening, worried about going home, worried about missing his friends, worried about the next school. And she knew he'd miss Ashley; was probably a little resentful that she got to stay and he didn't.

"Think the gold might be up there?" Mariah asked.

"Yeah." Brian swung a stocking foot. "That part's blocked off in the attic, so I couldn't look."

Mariah patted his knee as she walked past him to the refrigerator. "Someday you'll be a brilliant businessman and make your own money to do whatever you want with it. Want some milk?"

"No, thank you. I wonder if my mom will be home this summer or if she'll be working."

Mariah tried to remember what news Lavinia's last conversation with the woman had yielded. "I think she's doing another movie, but it's in L.A. It's about a boys' baseball team. She's going to get you a part as an extra.''

He made a face. "I've done that before. You wait around a long time in these dorky costumes, then all you do is walk by the camera or sit in a crowd. It's boring. When I grow up, I'm going to be a plumber.''

Mariah bit her lip to withhold a smile. Did Cam know he was creating competition for himself by being the children's hero?

"That'd be an excellent career choice,'' she encouraged. "You're smart enough to make a good life for yourself, Brian.''

He sighed. "Yeah, that's what Cam said. That I'll be eighteen before I know it and can decide things for myself.''

"That's right.''

He sighed. "Still seems to me that eight years is a really long time.'' With that, he slithered off the counter, hugged her good-night and went up to bed.

Her heart ached.

She went upstairs to do her final tuck-in, then was on her way back downstairs when the doorbell rang.

She pulled the door open to find Parker standing there, a frown pleating her forehead. "Married?'' she said without preamble, storming past Mariah and into the house. "You're getting *married* and you didn't tell me?''

Mariah shushed her. "I just got the kids to bed.

It's a complicated story. I tried to call you this morning, but you didn't answer your cell, and there's been so much going on since that I sort of…forgot.''

Refusing to be placated, Parker stood her ground. Wearing a yellow sweatshirt over black leggings, with a giant fabric pouch made of quilt squares over her shoulder, she was hard to ignore. "You forgot. If Rita Robidoux hadn't waited on me at the Barn, I still wouldn't know!''

Mariah arched an eyebrow. "Rita knew? It just happened this—''

"Rita works for Perk Avenue's catering service on the side. They called her about a wedding reception Tuesday night—the Trent-Mercer wedding. Talk fast. Massage correctly applied can be lethal, you realize.''

Mariah gestured her to a corner of the sofa and microwaved the last two cups of coffee in the pot. Then she added Irish Cream to them.

Sitting beside Parker with a cushion between them, she explained about Ashley's guardian, Ashley's creative fib and her and Cam's decision to make the untruth a reality in order to save the child from foster care.

Parker looked worried. "But if you split up in a year, how is that going to help Ashley?''

Mariah didn't have an answer. "We're taking it day by day.''

"But…''

"Park, please. Just let it be as it is, okay?''

Parker smiled. "I rather like it as it is, I just wondered how you're going to cope. I presume you and Cam will be sleeping together?"

"If and when we feel ready."

"How can you look at him and not feel ready?"

Mariah pursed her lips at her sister. "Because that's not what I want."

"Now, that's an outright lie. You look at him as though he's *everything* you want."

"If I'd met him before Ben, he'd have been everything I wanted then. Now I know better, so I want different things. Haven't we had this discussion?"

Parker dropped her head against the back of the sofa. "Probably. You're very repetitious. You think you can't want him because you can't be what he wants, or some such idiocy. Frankly, I'm tired of discussing it. You can redeem yourself by telling me I'm your maid of honor."

"You're my maid of honor."

"All right, then."

MRS. MORRIS ARRIVED at 9:00 a.m. with a portly middle-aged man in an Italian suit and glasses. He was only slighter taller than she, and not at all who Mariah would have expected to interest the beautiful woman whose first husband had been a model.

He worked on Wall Street Monday through Friday, he explained to the girls, but had a farm in upstate New York, where they would all spend weekends.

They went from cautiously suspicious of him to excitedly hopeful when he told them about the horse on the farm and Missy, the golden retriever, who'd just given birth to thirteen puppies.

Mariah hugged the girls goodbye, delighted to see that the sadness of leaving was practically forgotten as they piled into the station wagon. Letitia and Lavinia were on hand to wave them off.

Brian and Ashley ran after them all the way to the road, still waving.

The Franklins pulled in shortly after.

Their mother was tall and California blond; their father, handsome and thickly built, looking precisely the way Mariah expected a stuntman to look.

"I can't believe Mom's really gonna act," Philip said, "instead of fall off stuff and wreck cars."

"Now that you two are getting older—" she wrapped an arm around each boy as her husband went into the house to get their things "—we thought it'd be nice if we were all in the same place at the same time."

Brian and the twins shook hands manfully, Mariah hugged them, the Lightfoot sisters embraced them and wished them well.

Silence seemed to fall when the car drove out of sight. Ashley and Brian stood together a little bit ahead of Mariah, staring at the spot where the car had disappeared from view.

"The Game Boy's still connected," Ashley said

to Brian. "You want to play until your mom comes?"

"I beat you all the time," he said dispiritedly as they turned to walk back to the house.

"That's 'cause I let you," Ashley said.

He made a scornful sound. "You do not."

"Come on," she said. "I'll show you."

"We're going back to my office," Letitia said, heading for the old Packard they'd driven from the school building. "Call me when Brian's mother arrives. We'd like to say goodbye."

"Of course."

Mariah went back into the house, made cocoa for Ashley and Brian, then busied herself cleaning out the refrigerator and straightening up the cupboards.

Shortly after two o'clock, she heard a car in the driveway and looked out the window, expecting to see a rental vehicle, which would mean Brian's mother had gotten there. Instead, she saw Cam's truck.

In a moment she heard him talking to Ashley and Brian. When she went out to greet him, the living room was empty. She peered around in surprise, then turned to a commotion at the top of the stairs. Ashley had a lamp from Mariah's room, Brian had a light wicker chair and Cam and a man she didn't recognize had a wooden chest she'd filled with clothes and linen.

"Mariah," Cam said as he and the other man

moved carefully down the stairs, "Evan Braga. Evan, Mariah Mercer."

Evan was about Cam's height, with dark-blond hair and dark-brown eyes. He was attractive in jeans and a paint-smeared sweatshirt, but there was a world-weary mien about him that touched her.

He smiled and inclined his head politely. "Hello," he said. Then he blew her first impression of him by adding, "I can't believe you're marrying this guy. Do you know about his fanatical devotion to baseball and his fascination with the old Chandler Mill building?"

That caught her interest. She met them at the bottom of the stairs. "I love the old Chandler Mill building. Cam said you two might buy it. Did you?"

"We did," Cam said. He and Evan picked up their pace as they crossed to the door. "The owner was so eager to get out from under that Evan got us a real deal. He put up the money."

Evan grinned. "Well, I'm counting on your smarts to make us a fortune."

She followed them out to the truck. "You're not going to tear it down, right? I mean, you said you'd fix it up."

Cam gave her an impatient glance as they placed her trunk on a padded tarp in the truck bed. "Of course we're not going to tear it down. We have a few tenants. We want to convert it to office space downstairs but use the upstairs for apartments."

She thought about that. "I'll bet the view of the lake from the upstairs rooms is wonderful."

He nodded. "And the construction's solid. It just needs remodeling inside to outfit it for residential spaces, and a time-appropriate face-lift outside."

Evan grinned. "I think this makes us entrepreneurs, or slum landlords. I'm not sure which."

Mariah noticed the empty cab of the truck. "Where's Fred?" she asked.

"I left him home," he replied. "Having him run around our feet while we're trying to move you wouldn't be a good thing. And he has a fenced yard on the side of the house, and a dog door for getting in and out. He's in heaven after the apartment." He caught her hand and pulled her with him toward the house. "Now, could we have more moving and less chatter?"

She frowned teasingly at Evan. "I can't believe you want to be in partnership with this man."

Evan blinked at her. "You're entering into the ultimate partnership with him. At least I don't have to look at his ugly mug at night."

Night. She felt a frisson of anxiety.

Or was it anticipation?

When the truck was loaded, the children pleaded to go with Cam.

"What if your mother arrives while you're gone?" she asked Brian.

He saw her point but looked bitterly disappointed. He was clearly enjoying the male companionship.

"I'll have him back in half an hour," Cam bargained. "The house is only five minutes away. We'll just unload and come right back."

"Okay," she conceded, then cautioned the children, "but you two be careful. And please do as you're told."

They raced each other toward the truck—an action she took optimistically as consent.

"Don't worry," Cam said. "We'll be right back."

"I'll have coffee and brownies ready."

"All *right!*" Cam gave her a quick kiss and a grin. "This relationship is looking hopeful already."

IT WAS DINNERTIME. Cam and Ryan and the children had been back for brownies, left again and made yet another trip, and there was still no sign of Brian's mother.

Letitia and Lavinia had come to the carriage house to wait, and they all now sat around the dining room table eating pizza Cam had ordered.

Brian had adopted a nonchalance Mariah found difficult to watch.

The scenario was all so familiar to Cam from his own childhood. How many times had he waited to be picked up from a school function or some other outing, only to be left sitting on his sports bag or leaning against a public telephone because no one came and no one answered the phone?

Brian was doing the same thing he always did—

pretending it didn't matter. The way Cam used to pretend that he wasn't so tired of his life he'd do anything to get out of it. Suicide had crossed his mind once, but he'd immediately rejected it, certain that when he was in control of his own life, things would be different. Besides, a permanent solution to a temporary problem was stupid.

But at ten, eighteen seemed like a lifetime away.

Letitia went into the living room to call Brian's mother to find out why she was delayed.

Mariah looked ready to blow up. She got up to refill everyone's glasses and to give the children more napkins.

Ashley was uncharacteristically quiet, obviously unsure what to do for Brian.

Cam glanced at the clock. He'd promised Evan he'd have him at his place by seven for a poker game.

He pushed his chair away from the table. "If you'll excuse us," he said, "I have to get Evan home. But I'll be back in fifteen minutes."

There was a desperate look in the boy's eyes as he pleaded with Mariah, "Can I go, too?" She prepared to reply, her expression reluctant, and he interrupted with "You know she's not coming. You'll have to put me on a plane tonight, and Bianca— that's her personal assistant," he added for Cam's benefit, "will pick me up at the airport."

Mariah turned to Cam.

"Fine with me. Let's go."

Mariah shook Evan's hand and thanked him for his help with a bag of brownies.

Cam pretended hurt feelings. "None for me?"

"Now that you're going to be my husband," she said heartlessly, walking them out to the porch, Ashley beside her, "you're required to help me without expecting payment."

"Really. Well, that's a misconception we'll have to straighten out when I return."

Evan lived in a cottage in the woods on the other side of town. He had a big family somewhere in the Midwest, and had come East to escape their well-intentioned hovering after an automobile accident that killed his brother and left him in the hospital for months.

He ran Lake Road with Hank regularly, and Cam found it hard to see that he'd ever had a physical problem. He played basketball on the team most of the Wonders belonged to, and pickup games at the gym. There was a determination about him, despite his easygoing manner, that spoke of a hard fight back to health and fitness.

He never volunteered much and Cam didn't ask. He understood a man's right to privacy.

"Thanks for the help," he said as Evan leaped out of the truck.

"Sure." Evan reached in to shake hands with Brian. "Good luck, Brian."

"Thanks." Brian slid onto the far edge of the seat as Evan closed the door and gave them a final wave.

"Nice guy," Brian said.

"Yeah," Cam agreed. He turned around in the small gravel drive, then headed down the narrow road through the woods to the main road.

They drove in silence halfway back to the Manor, then Brian said with a sigh, "My mom forgot me."

"It's hard to tell what happened," Cam said diplomatically. "We'll just have to wait and see if Miss Lightfoot can find out why she isn't here."

The boy sighed again. "She probably got high and just forgot me. It's happened before."

Cam thought the responsible, adult thing would be to discourage this kind of thinking. But caseworkers had done that to him his entire life, and it had never altered the underlying truth. Some people could be rehabilitated and some people couldn't.

Maybe it would be more responsible to help Brian see that he could survive his childhood. "My parents did that to me all the time, too."

Brian turned slightly toward him. "What did you do?"

"I made sure I survived to get out of there. And I was lucky. I got in with a great foster family."

Brian was silent a moment. "I never get taken away when my mom goes into rehab," he said finally. "'Cause Bianca's there. And it'd be bad publicity if my mom lost me. But once Bianca gets me back home, she doesn't show up again until Mom's out. Usually, it's just me and the housekeeper. She's very nice, but she'd old and she can't do much fun stuff.''

"Stinks, doesn't it?"

"Big time."

Darkness had fallen by the time they reached the carriage house. Letitia was on the porch to meet them.

"Oh-oh," Brian said.

"Don't borrow trouble," Cam advised.

Brian gave him a grim look. "I don't have to. I own a whole bunch of it."

"What happened, Miss Letty?" Brian asked as they approached the house.

Letitia said with her usual positive approach, "Well, you were right, Brian. Your mother isn't coming. Let's go inside and I'll explain. Cam?" She pointed him around the side of the house. "Mariah's in the garden."

It didn't occur to him to question why she was in the garden in the dark. This was Mariah, after all.

He heard her before he found her under a giant maple. It took an instant to adjust to the knowledge that she was crying; she was always so tough, so determined. Except where the children were involved. And he was sure that was what was prompting her tears now.

He went to her.

She turned at the sound of his footsteps and walked into his arms, just as she'd done Sunday night on the dance floor. But this was grief, not romance.

"What happened?" he asked, wrapping his arms around her.

"She did it again!" she said angrily, sobbing. "I can't believe it! How can you have a child and care so little about what…"

"Mariah. Did what again?"

She swallowed. "She had an accident on her way to the airport. Hit another car. Multiple injuries, but no deaths, thank God. Cocaine in her blood. This time it's not just rehab. She's facing criminal charges."

"Oh, God."

"Yeah. Bianca called." Mariah stood back, swiped a hand across her eyes, spread her arms and dropped them in complete exasperation. "And in the crush of things, everybody forgot about Brian. Do you believe it?"

He nodded. "I do."

She sighed, turned away, turned back, her fingers linked and twisting with a nervousness he'd never seen in her.

He waited.

"Bianca wanted to know if the school could keep Brian over the summer," she finally blurted, "until she learns what'll happen to his mother."

He saw where this was going and thought God seemed to be coming out on his side in this relationship.

"What did you tell her?"

"Letitia talked to her. She said the school was closed for the summer." More tears slid down her cheeks. She wiped them away impatiently. "That we could send someone home with Brian, but then she'd have to make arrangements for him. And if his mother goes to jail, they'll have to be long-term."

He nodded, remembering his conversation with Brian on the way home. "So even the kind but elderly housekeeper won't do this time."

"No."

The good thing about having few options, he'd always thought, was the time saved in deliberation.

"Okay," he said. "You call her back and I'll put Brian's stuff in the truck."

He turned away to do just that, but she caught his arm and turned him back to her.

She leaped onto him, her cheek wet against his as she wrapped her legs around him. "Thank you," she whispered tearfully in his ear. "Thank you, Cam."

He started toward the house with her. "Just remember, I'm doing this without having received any extra brownies."

"I'll make you brownies every day for a year."

A year. There was that deadline.

He pushed it from his mind, preferring to think that by the time it came around, it would be forgotten.

Letitia met them at the door, took one look at

Mariah's unorthodox position and said with a smile at Cam, "I'll call Bianca."

Brian needed more convincing than Bianca.

"Where am I going?" he wanted to know, as Cam carried a stack of his boxes to the truck.

"Home with us," he replied, not sure how he'd receive the news, uncertain what Letitia had told him about his mother and the accident.

"For how long?"

"Until things are decided." That was ambiguous enough. "Probably most of the summer, anyway."

The boy made a sound that was difficult to interpret in the dark. "You mean...at *your* house?"

"Yeah."

"With Mariah and Ashley. And Fred."

"Yeah."

That sound again. "My mom hurt some people in an accident."

"So I heard." Cam put the boxes in the bed of the truck, then headed back to the house. Brian kept pace with him. "But that doesn't have anything to do with you."

"She screws up all the time, but it's like she can't do anything about it."

"I know. Same kind of parents, remember?"

"I'm not going to be like that."

"I know."

They'd reached the house and Brian stopped in his tracks. Cam stopped with him.

"And I really get to live with you?" the boy

asked. His amazement was flattering. Cam wished that Mariah was infected with the same enthusiasm.

"For now. We'll have to see what happens when your mother's case is decided."

"Man. This is like Amy's princess book."

With a weird sense of life being in control of him instead of the other way around, Cam drove home half an hour later to his new house on the lake with his fiancée at his side and two kids in the jump seat.

CHAPTER THIRTEEN

CAM'S HOUSE WAS BEAUTIFUL, but Mariah had to view it while contending with Fred trying to kiss her face. Until he noticed the children, trailing behind with their sleeping bags. He pounced on them and they dissolved into laughter in the middle of the living room floor. She looked up, the dramatic vaulted ceiling snagging her attention. Then she caught sight of the sign Cam had bought from her hanging over the doorway to the kitchen. Live Well, Laugh Often, Love Much.

Cam led Mariah through a living room so large it had two conversation areas and two sets of furniture, one with deeply upholstered green-and-beige check sofa and chairs, another with chairs in a coordinating fabric. He pointed toward the kitchen, then beckoned her to follow him upstairs.

"My room's downstairs," he said, and motioned to the right side of the hallway. "Rooms for the kids." He indicated the two rooms side by side, flipping on lights.

"Everything's furnished," she said in amazement. "I mean, considering you just bought it..."

"Hank left a lot of the furniture because Jackie's place is full of her family's antiques."

"That's lucky, since none of the bedroom furniture at the Manor was ours. I thought the kids would have to use their sleeping bags until we could buy them furniture."

"Your room." He crossed to the large room on the left side of the hall and turned on the light. "Bathroom off each room. You have a fireplace, but just a shower, no tub. There's one in my bathroom, though. You can use it anytime."

Mariah walked into a spacious bedroom with soft yellow walls, large oak furniture, lace curtains and a pastel bedspread. A small escritoire stood in a corner, with a ladder-back chair pulled up to it, and next to it, a small, marble-framed fireplace.

"Overlooks the garden and the lake," he said, as she held a hand up to shield her eyes and peer out the window. "Not very much of a garden, but we can work on that over the summer if you want to."

"All I've ever done is plant a window box," she laughed.

"I haven't even done that. We can always call Gary Warren if we get desperate. Maybe we'll even get a deal since he's seeing your sister."

Mariah crossed the room to examine the wardrobe closet and found one that you could wander into, with hanging rods at different heights, built-in cubbyholes, a shoe rack. She stood back and gasped.

"What?" he asked, coming to check the closet, thinking something was wrong.

"My closet is bigger than the room I slept in as a child." She smiled in sheer feminine delight. "How fabulous is this?"

"If all your clothes are in that trunk, you'll have to do a lot of shopping to fill it up."

She shrugged blissfully. "I don't even have to fill it up. I just have to know everything won't get crushed when I hang it up. Hooks for hats, shelves for boxes, racks for shoes. I can't believe it!"

"I can go you one better," he taunted, catching her hand and taking her with him downstairs. "My room has a special fireplace."

"Special?"

"Yes." He led her into the huge blue-green-and-gold room done in Black Watch wallpaper, dark-blue woodwork and pine furniture. He pointed to the fireplace outlined with green tile and topped with a large slab of pine.

"I thought mine was wonderful, but this is gorgeous!" She put a hand to her heart. "I'll bet that's wonderful on a February night."

The image that sprang to mind as she spoke featured him beside her under the covers.

"But the best part," he said, tugging her around the corner and into the large bathroom, "is that it can be used in both rooms."

"Oh!" She sank onto the wide edge of the tub opposite the fireplace. In this room it had a country styling to match the decor. "I love to soak in a tub, but since I've been at the Manor, the best I could manage was a quick shower in the morning before I woke everybody up."

"Well, feel free to use this one anytime."

There was uproarious giggling and loud barking coming from the living room. Mariah got to her feet. "I'd better make sure they're not wreaking havoc. They're great kids, but they get a little careless when they're excited."

Fred had pinned Ashley to the carpet and she was beside herself with laughter while he licked her cheeks. Brian sat nearby, urging the dog on.

"Come and see your bedrooms," Mariah said, having to fend off the dog, who ran to her the moment he saw her.

She fussed over him, then followed with him as Cam led the way upstairs and showed the children the two rooms. "Can you come to a peaceful agreement over who gets which?"

Together, Ashley and Brian peered into the first one, done in paneled walls, with large blue-and-white plaid bedspread and drapes. Then they checked the second one, done in large pink-and-blue flowers and white furniture. This room definitely had a feminine twist. Cam must have thought so, too, Mariah noted, spotting Ashley's boxes in a corner.

"The other one's for me," Brian said, going back to it immediately, the dog still following him.

Ashley walked into the flowered room and stared

out the long window. "What's out there?" she asked.

"The lake," Cam answered. "You can see it from Brian's window, too. It has a deck outside that runs the whole length of this side of the house."

Her eyes were huge. "We can have picnics out there!"

He nodded. "That's the plan. I made up the beds this morning, so you can jump in whenever you're ready. I'm going to get the rest of Brian's stuff."

"I'll help you." Mariah prepared to go, too, but Brian stood in Ashley's doorway, Fred at his side.

"I'll help," he said. "It's my stuff."

While heavy male footsteps and laughter traveled from the room next door to the garage and back again, Fred barking in tune with them, Mariah helped Ashley put her things away.

"I can't believe Brian and I got here," Ashley said, shaking her head. "And he didn't even have to find the gold."

"Sometimes," Mariah said, putting shorts and shirts in a drawer, "we get lucky and life gives us good things."

Ashley bristled at the suggestion that she'd gotten lucky. "It's because I took charge. I knew how I wanted it, and I made it happen, just like the Gypsy said. You're getting married! I have parents again and I'm going to be a really good daughter. When you're old, I'm going to buy you expensive presents from my travels with the ballet company."

Mariah couldn't take issue with the young girl. The simple truth was, Ashley was right. The complicated truth—a conflicted woman, a generous man—was too daunting to think about right now.

Mariah laughed and handed her a towel. "Don't wait until I'm too old."

While Ashley showered, Mariah turned her bed down, then went to check on Brian. He had put his clothes away and was placing a collection of race car models on his windowsill.

"Everything okay?" she asked. He hadn't said much about his mother when Letitia had told him about the accident, except to ask if she was going to be all right. When Letitia assured him that she would, but that she might have to go to jail, he'd nodded. "The housekeeper used to talk to Bianca about it. She said someday my mother was going to kill herself or somebody else. I'm glad nobody died."

It was a generous thought, yet a pathetic reason for a child to be grateful.

He turned to smile at her, looking weary. "I'm good. This is a cool room. My one at my mom's is really big and has a bunch of stuff in it, but this one feels just right.

"And he's pretty cool," Brian said. There was no need to explain who he was talking about.

She had to agree with that. "Where is he?"

"He said he had to make a few calls. He's got this desk in the kitchen, where he does his stuff for graduate school.'' He looked amazed. ''Imagine *wanting* to go to school that long.''

''He has plans he thinks he could better accomplish with a degree. His life was pretty rough when he was a kid.''

''Yeah, he told me. It's funny that he'd finally get rid of all of his problems and still want to have kids around with sort of the same problems he just got rid of.''

Mariah hugged Brian, giving him credit for powers of observation beyond his years. ''Shower before you go to bed, okay? It'll help you sleep better.''

''Okay.''

''I'll be back to tuck you in.''

He rolled his eyes. ''We're not at the school anymore. And I'm ten. You don't have to tuck me in.''

''What if I just look in and say good-night?''

''That'd be okay.''

Mariah went downstairs to make something hot to drink and Fred stayed with Brian.

Cam, seated on an overstuffed sofa across the room, waved at her as he spoke on a cordless phone.

''Yeah, that'd be great,'' he said as she found a kettle on the stove and searched the cupboards for tea. ''No, I don't expect you to be here for the wedding, I just thought I should let you know. I'll send you pictures. Yeah, there's plenty of room. If you guys can come later in the summer, we'd love to have you. The boys would like it here. And I've got an old boat for fishing on the lake.''

Mariah found a box of chamomile tea and winced—she'd almost rather go without, but not quite. She took down the box, then prayed she could locate some honey to blunt the taste. She held the jar of it to her chest in gratitude when she did. "Thank you!" she whispered prayerfully.

"You're welcome," Cam said as he appeared beside her. "What did I do?"

She took the kettle to the sink and filled it. "Actually, I was thanking the fates for honey, but you're probably the one who bought it."

"I am. What are you putting it on?"

"In," she corrected him, then held up the box. "My tea."

"Hank left that." He made a face. "He didn't like it and I pretty much agree."

She placed the kettle on the burner and turned it on. "I do, too, but it's better than nothing. Tomorrow I'll buy some black tea."

"Make a list of what you and the kids need and I'll take you shopping. Unless there's a plumbing crisis somewhere, then you're on your own. My brother's thinking of visiting at the end of the summer. You'll like him. His wife had four little boys when he married her."

She smiled. "Another knight in shining armor?"

He laughed lightly. "Yeah. Runs in the family." He asked as an afterthought, "Do you cook?"

"Yes," she was happy to reply. "I'm not brilliant, but I'm not bad. And I did promise you brownies.''

He nodded, the air changing subtly between them. She felt her skin prickle, her pulse quicken.

''Every day for the whole year,'' he reminded her, leaning against the counter with both disbelief and amusement in his eyes. ''I suppose I should have gotten that in writing.''

''I'm true to my word. But I have some other treats you might want to sample.''

By the time she heard the words come out of her mouth, it was too late to edit them. And in the change of atmosphere in the corner of the kitchen, they sounded particularly suggestive.

''I make a mean lemon meringue,'' she added quickly, feeling the color creep up from her neckline. She didn't understand it. She'd been married for four years. There was no reason to be embarrassed by sexual innuendo. ''Strawberry shortcake, peanut butter pie, chocolate chip cake with cooked…'' She'd have listed the entire contents of the dessert section of her cookbook if he hadn't stopped her abruptly by taking her chin in the vee of his thumb and forefinger.

He concentrated on her with languid hazel eyes, then lowered his mouth to take hers. He was fairly quick, though that kiss reached right into her soul.

''What was that for?'' she asked breathlessly when he released her.

He smiled in self-deprecation. ''Because you're

cute when you're embarrassed. I apologize if that sounds sexist, but it's honest. You're always so controlled that it was fun to see you in a fluster.''

''Ready, Mariah!'' Ashley shouted from beyond the hallway before Mariah could react or reply.

''Ready for what?'' Cam asked.

''For tucking in.''

''You still do that at this age?''

She shrugged, trying to reestablish equilibrium. ''I always did because they were away from home and I wanted them to feel safe and cherished. But Brian told me just a few minutes ago that he's too old for it. Maybe you should tell him good-night. He won't resent it coming from you.''

''Sure,'' he said, following her up as she went toward Ashley's room. He stopped at Brian's.

Brian sat up in bed, holding in his hands the globe that normally stood on a built-in shelf. Fred, who'd been lying across Brian's feet, ran to Cam.

''Going somewhere?'' Cam asked, indicating the globe.

''No.'' Brian gave the globe a spin, his expression thoughtful. Fred barked at the suspicious movement and went closer to sniff.

''I was just thinking how cool it is that there are all these faraway places full of interesting stuff that I just don't care about. No, I don't mean I don't *care* about them—I just mean I don't care if I *see* them. 'Cause I like it right here.''

He scrambled out of bed to put the globe away, then climbed back under the covers.

The kid, Cam thought, was remarkable.

"You warm enough?"

"Yeah, thanks."

"Found the towels okay?"

"Yeah."

"We're making a list to go shopping tomorrow. Anything you need?"

He reflected, then asked, "Is model car glue a need?"

"Absolutely. I always need anchovies."

Brian crossed his eyes and made a horrible face.

Cam laughed and resisted a surprising impulse to straighten his blankets. It didn't take long, he realized, for children to take over your mind.

He turned out the light. "Sleep well. Holler if you want anything."

As Cam backed out of the room, he collided with Mariah, peeking in. She caught his arm to steady herself.

"Good night, Brian," she called.

He replied, already sounding sleepy.

"'Night, Cam," Ashley shouted.

"Good night, Ashley."

Fred couldn't decide whether to stay or go, but then he followed Cam.

Mariah maintained her hold on Cam's arm as they walked together back down to the kitchen. The kettle was whistling.

She took it off the burner and made her tea. "Can I fix you anything?" she asked.

He knew he couldn't be around her tonight and maintain his sanity. She was wearing pink cotton sweats, and since they'd gotten home, she'd brushed her hair out. She was smiling and relaxed. He could only guess that it was because she finally had what she wanted, though not in the way she'd intended to get it.

Instead of babies, she had two ten-year-olds, and though they had no idea what would happen to Brian eventually, for now she had her two children.

Whatever the reason, she appeared ripe and seductive. Her baggy clothes hid nothing, clinging to her probably bare breasts and her sweet round backside. She was small and perfect, and if he succumbed to impulse, he'd make love to her until he'd wiped Europe from her mind.

He shook his head and moved over to the sofa. Fred sank onto the carpet in front of it. "Thanks. But I'm taking a computer course over the summer and I've got some reading to do."

She came toward him, determination in her eyes. The air changed as it had before. Electricity made his heart stutter and almost fail.

She put a hand to his arm. "I am so grateful for your willingness to help the children."

"I don't think anyone could have turned away," he said. He felt weak. Wanted to take a step back, out of her reach, but there was something wonderful about the torture of her touch.

"Nine men out of ten would have," she said, her voice softening. "Probably 99 out of 100."

He saw it in her eyes—affection born out of gratitude. He wasn't sure he was strong enough to do what he had to.

He crossed his arms in an unconscious attempt to ward her off, but she put a hand to his wrist, her index finger rubbing gently, silkily, over the bone there. "What if I told you," she asked, her voice a whisper, "that I was so *inclined?*"

In his fantasy, he caught a fistful of her hair, kissed her senseless, swept her up in his arms and took her to bed.

In reality, he knew he had to fight for a better foundation for this marriage. He drew a breath, hating himself, and replied quietly, "I'd say that as desperately as I've longed to hear that from you, I'd prefer it under different conditions."

She blinked at him, momentarily more shocked than embarrassed.

"I want this marriage to be about us, not about them. I'm happy to have them—don't misunderstand me—but I'd have done my damnedest for them without you, and I'd have moved heaven and earth to get you to marry me whether or not they'd been in the picture."

She closed her eyes for a moment, then opened them and faced him squarely. "Let me get this straight,'' she began in a strangled voice. ''You said when I asked you to marry me that you weren't going to have a marriage without sex. Or did I imagine that?''

Fred sat up, unhappy about the change of atmosphere.

His arms still crossed so that he wouldn't abandon his lofty position and grab her, anyway, Cam said, ''Well, Mariah, you're missing a subtle difference here.''

She put her hands on her hips, growing angry. ''Do tell. What am I missing?''

''I said I didn't want a marriage without love-making.''

She shook her head in exasperation. ''You think I don't know the difference?''

He drew a breath, hoping the oxygen would help him reason clearly. ''No, but I think you think *I* don't know the difference.''

While she took a moment to ponder that, he went on. ''This would have been thank-you sex, rather than love-from-the-bottom-of-your-heart sex.''

She stared at him, absorbing that, then spread her arms and said, ''Cameron, I don't believe you!''

He ran a hand over his face, feeling as though every system in his body was working backward because rejecting her was contrary to his every inclination. ''Neither do I,'' he sighed.

''You're actually turning me down.''

''No, I'm not. I'm holding out for better terms.''

Fred whined. Cam felt like whining, too.

She reached to the counter for her cup of tea. "Well, I hope you have patience and endurance, because it'll be spring in Outer Mongolia before I feel so inclined again. Good night."

She walked away.

He reminded himself that putting off immediate gratification in the hope of working toward a more permanent fulfillment later was really a noble thing.

It didn't help.

CHAPTER FOURTEEN

CAM AND MARIAH'S WEDDING was supposed to be a simple affair, but the Lightfoot sisters got carried away. Cam guessed that only the time constraint prevented them from booking New York's Plaza Hotel and asking Luciano Pavarotti to sing.

As it was, they were married at the Maple Hill Methodist Church, with Mariah in an ice-blue gown Jackie lent her and with a veil Addy made.

Parker and Ashley were dressed in dark blue, their hair done up with small white flowers. Cam, Hank and Brian wore suits they'd bought in Springfield the day before.

Jackie and Hank hosted the reception at the Yankee Inn.

Mariah couldn't believe how many people attended.

"They're all friends of Cam's," Jackie said, "or clients he's done work for. When word got out that you two took the kids in—well, Maple Hill's devoted to its children."

"But they don't even know me and look at that table of gifts!"

"Don't question. Just be grateful."

Grateful.

That word was beginning to have a worse effect on her than *escape* did. She stopped in her tracks every time she thought it, and she'd thought it a lot as Parker, the Lightfoot sisters, Jackie, Haley and all the Wonders had rallied the last few days to put this wedding together.

She had intended the lovemaking she'd proposed to Cam to be about gratitude. As she thought about it in hindsight, she decided it would have put her in a superior position. She'd have taught him that giving her what she wanted would be beneficial to him.

Instead, he'd taught her that he welcomed the children for himself and not for her, and that if she thought offering him sex would bend him to her will, she was mistaken.

Coming to that conclusion had taken her three days. And during that time, they'd seen very little of each other. He'd been working day and night on the kitchen at the Manor to make sure it was ready for the crew putting up wallboard on Wednesday.

She'd spent the days finding things for the children to do, signing them up with the Parks and Recreation Department's various sports and craft projects, learning about the house, preparing meals.

Cam usually grabbed dinner on the run, but he never failed to thank her for it or tell her it was delicious. The children were all over him for the brief time he was home, but he dealt with them patiently, laughing with them over reports of Fred's antics.

The dog was a devoted companion and personal comedy act all in one. He chased the children, then ran from them to encourage their pursuit. He mooched treats in a style Cam insisted wasn't begging but highway robbery.

Whenever Mariah sat, Fred sat beside her with his head in her lap or on her feet.

It had been only three days, she mused as she watched Cam with their guests, and she was in love with their life. And, God help her, she was in love with him. She didn't want to be, had fought it with everything in her, but his determination to love her was stronger than her ability to resist him.

This felt very different from the love she'd had for Ben. That had been warm and sweet and hopeful—but turned out to be cold and unforgiving, with every hope dashed.

What she felt for Cam was hot and had no sweetness about it. It felt bigger than she was, louder than her thoughts, stronger than her own life force.

She could barely contain it and had to admit—if only to herself—that she was almost afraid of it.

Jackie came to her with Ashley and Brian and two of her four children. "The kids and I have talked it over," she said, "and your two are spending the night with us."

"But you have four of your own!"

"That'll only make it more fun. Ashley can sleep

with the girls, and Brian can bunk on the couch. The twins are too loud for anyone to sleep with.''

''Well…are you sure?'' Mariah felt a sense of panic. Jackie was trying to give her a wedding night. ''Maybe we should check with Cam.''

''We already have,'' Ashley said, looking excited. She was flanked by Jackie's girls, who were giggling. ''He says it's okay if it's okay with you.''

''Good.'' Without waiting for an answer, Jackie shooed the children toward the cake table. She sniffed the small nosegay Mariah carried. ''You can throw your bouquet and take off any time you want. Try to aim this at Parker. She and Gary are looking pretty serious.''

Mariah looked across the room where Cam had been and found him wending his way through the crowd toward her.

''Are you ready to go?'' she asked.

''Any time you are,'' he replied.

Jackie clapped for everyone's attention, then beckoned all the single women forward. There was laughter and jostling as some took positions in the back, hiding behind while others took offensive positions in front.

Jackie offered her hand to help Mariah stand on one of the dining room chairs.

Mariah spotted Parker in the crowd, playfully fighting Glory Anselmo, Jackie's nanny and Jimmy Elliott's girlfriend, for a front spot. Mariah turned and tossed the small bouquet over her shoulder in

Parker's direction. There were screams and squeals and when she turned back round, Glory and Parker each had a piece of it, both women laughingly refusing to let go.

Until Gary appeared to kiss Parker, who suddenly seemed to forget her need for the bouquet.

Glory screamed and leaped in the air with it, waving it triumphantly over her head. Jimmy caught her to him, laughing.

Mariah looked for Jackie to help her down, but found Cam, instead. Rather than offer his hand, he bracketed her waist and swept her to the floor.

"Where's everybody going?" she asked. A general exodus was under way. At the door, they all flanked the long walkway from the church to the street.

"This must be the rice gauntlet," Cam speculated.

"Not rice. Birdseed," Mariah corrected him, remembering that Jackie had had everyone at city hall making the little bags on their lunch hours.

Cam looked puzzled. "I didn't know birdseed promised fertility."

"It doesn't," she explained. "But the birds eat it, so rice doesn't litter the street."

"So the significance of the ritual's just lost?"

"Relax," she said. "It wouldn't have worked with me, anyway. You ready?"

He caught her hand and started forward. "Am I ready!"

CAM TOOK OFF HIS TIE as he drove them home in Mariah's van—a more reputable vehicle for a special occasion than his truck. It was now dark and cool, the fragrance from the open window a mixture of woods and wildflowers.

She leaned her head back against her seat, her veil in her lap. Jackie and Haley had helped her wind her hair into a knot, and she now shifted uncomfortably on it. Finally, she pulled out the pins and combed out the dark, glossy mass with her fingers.

Her hair was magnificent, he acknowledged for the umpteenth time since he'd met her. He had to make himself concentrate on the road.

She seemed different today, more mellow and relaxed despite the festive ceremony, but it didn't mean anything would change tonight. He accepted that.

At least he'd dealt with it philosophically most of the day. But now, with her resting languidly in her seat beside him and the perfume of fecund summer all around them, to continue deluding himself was hard. He wanted her desperately.

The house, when they arrived, was dark and filled with that same fragrance of promise. They'd left the windows open on the lake side and the sound of lapping water greeted their arrival.

He locked the door behind him, intercepted Fred's assault of ecstatic welcome while Mariah sidestepped the dog to save Jackie's dress.

"Be right back!" she called as she ran for the

hallway. "Evan left a bottle of champagne when he dropped off his gift!"

That suggested she intended for him to open it. Hmm. He tossed his jacket on a chair and his tie after it, and undid the top two buttons of his shirt. Fred settled under the table.

The bottle opened with a satisfying pop. Lacking champagne flutes, he was pouring the wine into two water glasses when Mariah came up beside him in a long white slip. No, it was a negligee.

He forgot to stop pouring.

With a soft squeal of laughter, Mariah righted his hand and moved it and the overflowing glass to the sink. She sopped up the mess with a paper towel and glanced at him with unmistakable affection. He'd caught that glance a few times today while they'd been separated by well-wishing friends at their reception. He'd been sure he was imagining things.

She held the fluid silk of the negligee's skirt out and did a turn. It highlighted the curve of her hips and thighs, and through the openwork of the lace, he caught a glimpse of the rosy tips of her breasts. He couldn't speak.

"It was a gift from Letitia and Lavinia," she said, her fingertips running up the vee neckline to her white shoulder. "They're convinced we're going to fall madly in love."

A note in her tone suggested they were wrong. Now he was even more off balance.

"You're sure they're mistaken," he said.

"I know they're mistaken," she replied, holding up her glass. Then she added in a whisper he knew he'd remember until the day he died, possibly even after, "I've already fallen."

His heart stalled. Had she said that, or was he hallucinating?

She answered that by clinking her glass against his and toasting, "To us."

He drank to the toast. Then lifted her in his arms and carried her to his bedroom. Fred followed, watching with confused surprise as he was left on the wrong side of the door.

MARIAH COULDN'T BREATHE. For so long in her marriage to Ben, lovemaking had meant reproduction. The simple wonder of making love, the soul-stirring, mind-boggling impact of it, had been lost in the rigorous details and timing called for in the interest of conception. It had ceased to be about him or her.

Now Cam's every movement revered her. He set her gently on her feet by the side of his bed, removed the negligee carefully and draped it over the foot of the bed. Then he held her away from him and studied her with flattering seriousness.

His eyes finally met hers with admiration in them, and a possessiveness she felt all the way to her heart.

"You're very beautiful," he said softly.

She dismissed that with a shift of her shoulders

and was about to deny it verbally, when he put a hand to her waist and sensation ricocheted up her body and then down. She lost the power of speech.

He used that hand to draw her to him and then he simply held her. She wrapped her arms around him, knowing instinctively how critical the moment was, that making love would change everything.

"I love you," he said, hugging her to him.

She felt the buttons of his shirt embossing her skin, the fabric of his slacks rubbing the soft flesh on the inside of her thigh.

There'd been a time when she'd thought she'd never want to make love again. Now she couldn't wait to fill herself with him.

"I love you, too," she whispered against his collarbone. "Oh, Cam, I love you, too."

He lifted her to place her on the bed, then sat down to pull off his shoes and socks. She scrambled onto her knees to help him, lifting his shirt out of his slacks, unbuttoning buttons, tugging off his clothes. They finally lay together in the middle of the bed and settled into each other's arms.

Cam's hand traced the length of her body, trailing sparks over her shoulder, down her side, across her tummy.

She explored his back, finding the jut of his shoulder blades, the crenellated line of his spine, the muscled curve of his buttocks.

He pressed her close and turned so that she lay atop him. His hands explored every curve while she planted kisses across the dusting of hair on his chest, then down the middle of him to his navel.

With an intake of breath, he tipped her sideways into his arm and kissed the hollow of her throat. His hand swept along the inside of her thigh, then touched the now warm and pulsing heart of her.

She trembled.

He raised his head to look into her eyes, his turbulent with desire, yet somehow gentle. "You're shaking," he observed softly. "Is that good or bad?"

"It's good," she murmured.

"You have to tell me the truth."

"I am." She'd half expected to react negatively to the intimate touch. For so long her body had symbolized all her failures as a woman—all the babies she'd lost.

But this lovemaking was about her and him and the gift of this moment.

He cradled her in his arms and brushed the tumbled hair from her face. "Do you hate this part?" he asked, his thumb massaging her temple.

She was surprised by his perception. "I used to," she replied honestly. Then she smiled. "But I'm liking this very much. Please don't stop."

He whispered her name and touched her again, reaching inside her with an artistry that made looking backward a waste of time. She lost awareness of everything but the two of them; her world now the narrow space they occupied in the middle of the bed.

Even that seemed to dissolve as pleasure approached her, eluded her, then came upon her with the impact of a punch. Sensation throbbed inside her, so strong that she felt as though she'd gone headfirst off a cliff, only to land miraculously on a feather pillow as pleasure echoed and echoed again before drifting away.

She didn't want to think about gratitude, but that was what she felt. Not because Cam had given her pleasure, but because he'd restored her sense of the woman she'd felt sure had died with the last baby.

CAM WAS HAPPY, RELIEVED, that she was as invested in this effort to communicate as he was. She was so focused on him, made the softest, most desperate little sounds, then said his name on a gasp before pressing her face into his shoulder and dissolving into a long series of tremors.

He'd known they'd be good together. Later, he'd have to remind her that if she'd listened to him in the first place…

He lost the idea when she touched him.

He'd thought it would be nice to take her through it again so that she couldn't forget how right he'd been, but she had her own plan. And he wasn't man enough to resist.

Actually, he was, but her uses for his masculinity were more positive. Her soft touch ran over and over him until he had the intellect of an idiot but the sensitivity of an empath.

By the time he pushed her back against the pillows and rose over her, he felt he could see into her soul. Touch translated all the things there were no words for into feeling.

When he entered her and she welcomed him, it was as though a star had opened up and enveloped them. Brightness filled the space inside him and out and every bad thing that had ever happened to him faded into insignificance.

Mariah shuddered under him and he held her tightly as they fell back to reality together. But it was reality with a new truth to it. Love prevailed.

CHAPTER FIFTEEN

MARIAH HAD NEVER BEEN so happy. The month of June was like a fairy tale for adults.

Cam started work on the homeless shelter, a project that had been stalled for months but was now finally under way. She sent him off every morning with a bag lunch and a kiss after having lain in his arms all night.

On alternate mornings, she and Fred took the children to the park for their scheduled activities, stopped at the bakery, then hurried home to work on a painting she'd begun of a family on the beach.

She picked up the children midafternoon, then listened to their laughing and bickering and Fred's barking as they shot hoops outside, or heard the teenybopper voices on afternoon television when they stayed in. Either way, she found the cacophony a happy background as she prepared dinner. On weekends, they went for drives or barbecued at home, and Cam often took the kids and the dog fishing in the small boat tied up to their dock.

She couldn't quite believe how she and Ben had pursued this life and it had always been out of reach.

Then, when she'd been sure all hope of family life was lost to her, it had practically fallen on her from the sky. Well, Brian had, anyway.

Addy Whitcomb, who lived on the other side of the lake, hosted a Fourth of July picnic. The Megraths and Mike, Hank and Jackie and their children, Parker and Gary and his teenagers and Evan Braga sat on lawn chairs or on blankets on the rich grass that sloped down to the lake. Fred was beside himself with so much attention.

They ate and laughed all afternoon while the children and the dog chased one another until they were exhausted.

At dusk they had a last round of strawberry shortcake and settled down to listen to Gary's kids and Mike McGee, who were practicing several new numbers for the high school choir and tried them out on their willing audience.

Addy joined in, familiar with many of the old romantic ballads, then soon everyone else did, the music mellowing their moods. Families moved together into little knots, a part of the group yet separate, songs of love reminding them of their bond.

As Mariah leaned into Cam, with Ashley, Brian and Fred sprawled against them, she let herself be swallowed in the moment. Love and contentment closed over her head and she said a prayer of gratitude for the gift of her family.

It occurred to her that this *could* last forever.

Weary from their busy day's misadventures, the

children were asleep shortly after nine, Fred on his back on the foot of Brian's bed. The house was filled with the nighttime glow of a contented household.

Mariah found Cam in a tub filled with bubbles at nine-thirty, his arms beckoning her to him. There were candles on the windowsill and the wide rim of the tub.

She ripped off shorts, shirt and underwear, toed out of her shoes and climbed in to fit between his knees and lie back against him with an ''Aah!'' of bliss.

After a few moments of soaking, they soaped each other, scrubbed shoulders and backs with a loofah, then somehow lost the purpose of the bath…or found it.

Bubbles flew and floated on the candlelit air as they made love, lost in their continuing discovery of each other.

THE MIDDLE OF THE FOLLOWING week, the children were at classes at the swimming pool, and Cam was enjoying a day off. Mariah had just warmed blueberry muffins and made coffee, Fred glued to her heels, hoping for a handout. Bart Megrath had just stopped by and Mariah invited him to stay.

''I'd love to, but I can't.'' He glanced at his watch. ''I have court in half an hour. I know all Ashley's clothes and toys were shipped to you, but this box of legal paperwork was sent to my office.'' He handed it to Cam. ''I thought you should have it first, then if there's anything you want me to look over, let me know.''

Cam walked him out to his car while Mariah opened the box and pulled out several file folders. The tab on one of them read ''Ashley Weisfield's Adoption.''

Cam returned and read over her shoulder. ''Anything interesting?''

They sat at a right angle to each other and shared the pages in the file. Mariah gave Fred a muffin to move him out from between them.

She was trying to make sense of Walter Kerwin's notes in a mostly illegible hand, when Cam, looking at a long, legal document said, a startling note in his voice, ''Oh, my God!''

Mariah glanced up with a sense of foreboding. ''What?''

Cam stared at the document, sure he must have misread it. This couldn't be? What were the odds? Astronomical at best.

''What?'' Mariah demanded for a second time. She put her hand to his wrist. ''Cam, what's the matter? You're gray!''

He tried to think clearly. He held up a finger for silence so that he could reread the document. He had to be sure he wasn't misunderstanding this.

''Adopted father,'' it read, ''James Weisfield. Adopted mother, Eleanor Simms Weisfield.'' Okay, that was a surprise, but he understood it. Ashley had been adopted by the Weisfields, not born to them.

He looked at the bottom of the form, where Ashley's natural parents were listed. The name of the father was blank. He stared at the name of the mother again and felt the shock run through him and settle in the pit of his stomach.

He handed the form to Mariah.

She studied him worriedly as she took it. "What's wrong?"

"Ashley was adopted by the Weisfields," he said.

She nodded. "I know that. When she was a baby."

"Read the name of the natural mother," he said.

Mariah's eyes scanned the sheet. "Barbara Elizabeth Tr—" She stopped, her eyes widening, her mouth open in astonishment as she gazed up at him. "Barbara *Trent*." She swallowed. "Ashley is... yours?"

It hadn't occurred to him that she might think that. "No," he corrected her, rifling through the file for something that might offer an explanation. "Barbara was my sister. Ashley is my niece."

Mariah gasped. "But I can't believe...I mean, how could this have happened? The coincidence is..."

"We used to come here as children," he said, flipping through a sheaf of papers torn from a yellow pad. The handwriting was more legible and seemed to be a caseworker's notes. "Maybe Barbara came back here. We lost track of her for more than two years before she died."

"But the Weisfields were from New York."

He caught Barbara's name in some notes and laid the papers flat on the table. He went backward a page to find the beginning of the reference.

"'The Weisfields hired Barbara while summering in Maple Hill,'" he read aloud. "'She kept house for them and prepared meals, and they liked her so much they brought her back to New York with them in the winter. Their relationship was closer than that of employer-employee, and when she revealed that she was pregnant, they were already providing insurance but helped her with prenatal classes. Barbara and her child lived with them and Barbara continued working for them until her death in a motorcycle accident when Ashley was three months old.

"'I believe their bid to adopt Ashley is motivated by a genuine affection for the child and the child's mother. I support it wholeheartedly.'"

Cam leaned back in his chair, a storm of emotion inside him. He hated to think Barbara had stayed away because she'd been embarrassed that the modeling agency chose not to represent her or because she'd gotten pregnant.

But even as a little girl she'd been so sure of herself, so certain she was going to escape their lives and do big things.

He was comforted by the knowledge that before she died, Barbara had found people who cared for her and a place where she was happy. He was glad she'd had a child, if only for such a short time, so

that she'd known the familial love they'd all longed
for as children and never found—except in one another.

A gasp escaped him and Mariah came around the
table to wrap her arms around him. "Oh, Cam!"
she said, kissing his cheek. "Over all these years
and across all the miles and the convoluted paths
you and she have taken, you and Barbara are reconnected in…Ashley."

He heard an odd, new sound in Mariah's voice,
but he didn't dwell on it because he was consumed
with himself at the moment and his connection to
the child living under his roof.

Unaware of the blow he was dealing his marriage,
he said with the sincere wonder he felt, "I can't
believe it! Ashley is my own flesh and blood."

Mariah felt as if she'd been hit in the head with
a tire iron. Flesh and blood. You could deny its importance, convince yourself it really didn't matter,
but you couldn't fight instinct. Blood is thicker than
water. Blood calls to blood. Scores of aphorisms
about blood connections had survived the generations because their truth could not be disputed.

She was pleased for him, thrilled for Ashley because there wasn't a man the child loved more in
the world. But Mariah saw problems ahead for herself. Cam's joy at the discovery was genuine and
touching. He was ecstatic to have found his flesh
and blood.

How happy would Mariah be able to make him

in this marriage, she wondered anew, if he was just beginning to realize how important blood ties were?

The doorbell pealed urgently. Mariah went to answer it, happy to have an excuse to leave the room, misery moving in where only moments ago she'd felt so contented and secure.

Parker flew at her the moment she opened the door. She wrapped her in an herbal embrace, then stood back, beaming. Then she held up her left hand, the third finger bearing a silver band with a beautiful round-cut diamond in the center.

"We're getting married!" Parker stated the obvious, wrapping her arms around Mariah again. "Can you believe it? And the kids are happy about it, too! I don't know I got this lucky, but I'm not going to question it."

Mariah didn't have to force a smile, despite her own suddenly precarious happiness. She wanted very much for her sister to be happy. "That's so wonderful! We all love Gary and his kids. You got this lucky because he's a smart man and knows you're a wonderful woman. Have you set a date?"

"Two weeks from Saturday."

Mariah blinked. "That's pretty fast."

Parker rolled her eyes. "This from the woman who was married in four days." When Mariah conceded that with a nod, trying not to think about all that hung in the balance, Parker added, "You and Ashley and Stacey are wearing lavender. The three of us'll go shopping next week, okay? And we'll need Cam and Brian for groomsmen. I'll call you.'' She was already backing out the door. "I've got a million things to do. Kisses to Cam and the kids.''

"Bye!'' Mariah called after her as Parker ran out to her car. "Congratulations!''

"Congratulations to whom?'' Cam asked. "For what?'' He came up behind Mariah, tossing car keys on a ring on his index finger. He'd said earlier that he was going to stop by Hank's office to check next week's schedule, so he would pick up the children. He still looked a little stunned. Fred pranced, eager to accompany him.

"Parker,'' she replied. "She's getting married.'' Now she had to force the smile. She felt stiff and awkward, all the easy camaraderie of the past six weeks lost in her concern over an issue she'd thought settled.

She saw his eyes run over her face, as though he noted something wrong and was trying to figure out what it was.

"You're not happy about that?''

"I'm delighted,'' she replied, smiling wider, sure her pleasure must appear fake. "I love Gary. They'll be wonderful together.''

"Then what's the matter?''

"Nothing,'' she said. She sounded convincing to her ear, but he now knew every inch of her body and every subtle change in her emotions. He wasn't fooled. So she kept talking as she backed toward the kitchen, hoping he'd go out the door as he'd intended and she could collapse on a kitchen chair and have the breakdown she felt sure would be upon her any moment. "If you don't mind, while you're out, we need milk, eggs, bread and that juice stuff the kids like so much. You remember. We put vodka in it the other night when we ran out of tonic."

He was following her back to the kitchen and she was sure he hadn't heard a word of her impromptu grocery list. He was trying to read her eyes. At their heels, Fred looked anxiously from one to the other.

"You'll be late if you don't go now," she chattered, still backing away. "And you know Brian. If you aren't there on time, he'll find something outrageous to do, like drive a tractor home or..."

"They won't be out for half an hour."

"You were going to stop by the office first."

"I can do that after. Mariah." He drew her toward him as she tried to pull away. "What's the matter with you? You're not upset that Ashley's my...oh, God."

He understood; she saw it in his face.

His expression hardened, he dropped his hand and turned away from her, walking halfway toward the door, then turning back, temper igniting like kindling under a match.

"What is wrong with you, woman?" he asked.

"You know what's wrong with me!" she shot back, everything inside her churning into a ball of conflict and misery. "I'm not blaming you, Cam," she said, making an effort to remain calm, "but you just said it yourself. Ashley's your flesh and blood. That's why you're so happy you've found her. And you have every right to that.''

''Damn it, Mariah!'' he shouted. Fred whined and Cam ignored him. ''I'm happy because she's Barbara's flesh and blood, not because she's mine! She reconnects me with the sister I lost! We had such a grueling childhood that we were everything to each other. This is a little like having Barbara back.''

''I know,'' she insisted. ''Blood connections are important. I'm happy for you.''

He shook his head at her. ''Yeah. You look happy.''

She tried to make him see reason. ''Cam, I'll bet even you were surprised by how much it means to you that Ashley's your niece. We have fun together, and you generously agreed to shelter the kids—''

''Shelter them?'' he questioned hotly. ''I'm not sheltering them. We're adopting Ashley, and we're making a home for Brian until—''

''Cam, that's semantics! You agreed to marry me so I could adopt—''

''No.'' He cut her off quietly, but so abruptly that she felt it almost physically. ''I agreed to marry you because I wanted to marry you. And it was a wonderful bonus that Ashley was part of the deal.''

She tried one more time. ''Cam, you can *have* children.''

''I do have children,'' he said.

She sighed patiently. "One day they're going to make arrangements for Brian..."

"Maybe not. Maybe they'll let him stay here."

She'd harbored that hope, too, but it wouldn't help her argument at the moment.

"And when a year's up," she continued as though he hadn't spoken, "Ashley's coming to Europe with me. You should have children, Cam. Babies with your genes would be a wonderful addition to this world."

There. She'd cut him loose. She waited in anguish for him to take advantage of the opportunity.

CHAPTER SIXTEEN

CAM COULD NOT REMEMBER ever feeling so close to mayhem in his life. Even during his childhood years of neglect, then his wife's easy dismissal of him from her life, he'd never wanted to hurt anyone in return.

But to have the love he felt for Mariah and the children handed back to him was just about more than he could take.

He had to make contact. Much as he would have liked to throttle her, he settled for grabbing the collar of her shirt, instead. "Don't you dare pretend that you're nobly trying to give me my freedom, when we both know damn well what you're really doing."

Her wide eyes were blank. Was it possible she didn't really understand herself at all?

"I'm not the one who can't live without flesh-and-blood children," he said brutally, too hurt and angry to be diplomatic. "You are. So your infertility broke up your first marriage. That's sad. But instead of looking for someone who wouldn't care about it, you'd rather grieve for your lost babies by refusing to ever be happy with other children who need you even more. You'd rather be a martyr to the tragedy than be happy with me.''

She went pale.

He was still too angry to feel guilty. He freed her and turned away, afraid to be too close.

''You're the one who went after what you wanted,'' she said, her voice loud but tight, ''and was determined to hammer me into place where I didn't fit. You were ready to settle down, and you had to have me. I warned you—''

''Oh, stop it.'' He spun on her and went on without mercy. ''If you're going to tell me you warned me I'd want my own children one day, I don't want to hear it again. You are the most single-minded woman I've ever met. Which would be a good trait if you applied some sense to your determination. Well, you know what?'' He reached into his back pocket for his wallet, removed a credit card from it and slapped it into her hand. ''You're the one who should go. Go to Europe. Go to Bora Bora. Go wherever the hell you want, because I'm not about to spend a lifetime with you questioning my love at every turn.''

She was going to cry, but God forgive him, he had to get the rest of it out so that she knew he was as determined as she was.

''Bon voyage. If I'm still single when you return, look me up. Maybe the kids and I will take you back.''

Sudden horror filled her eyes. "If I go, I'm taking the children with me."

"I thought going to Europe was a mission of self-discovery."

"I've discovered," she countered, "that I want them."

He shook his head. "The state won't let you take Brian out of the country. He'll have to stay with me. And if you're going to put so much stock in flesh and blood, Ashley's mine, not yours. Our adoption is nowhere near final, so that's what the courts will have to go by."

"You wouldn't," she whispered.

He met her gaze and held it. "If you believe that, then you don't know me at all. I'm going to pick up the kids."

HE FELT AS THOUGH HE WAS dying. His heart was pounding, his head ached and he was having difficulty taking an even breath. Fighting down the need to scream bloody murder was taking its toll on him.

The kids were chattering away in the back seat. He glanced in the rearview mirror. Their faces were rosy from their strenuous morning of swimming. Brian's hair was spiky and wet; Ashley's was wound into precisely the same style of knot Mariah often wore. He couldn't live without those two kids. And he didn't know how he was going to live without Mariah. He could only pray she'd come to her senses. But every time he thought she had, this insanity about babies reared its head again.

He couldn't quite believe he'd told her to go. If she did, he'd have to be put on life support.

"We passed it!" the children whined in unison.

He pulled up at a red light, grateful that he'd even seen it in his state of mind. "Passed what?"

"Minuteman Ice Cream! You said we could stop."

"I did?"

Brian sounded puzzled. "We asked if we could get butterscotch sundaes and you said yes."

He turned his right blinker on. "Then we'll go back," he said.

When they got home, Mariah's van was still there, but there was no sign of her. He put the sundae the kids had insisted he buy her in the freezer and noticed that the credit card was gone. He was about to leave the children to finish their ice cream and wander through the house to see if he detected Mariah's presence, but Ashley noticed her name on the file folder on the table and sat down to look at the papers still spread there.

"What is all this stuff?" she asked, still working on her sundae. Brian had hiked up onto the counter to finish his.

Cam sat down opposite her. "It's some legal papers your guardian sent our lawyer. You know Mr. Megrath?"

"Yes. He's Rachel and Erica's uncle."

"Right. Well, he brought them over and I was looking through them. I found out something really interesting. And I thought it was neat."

She smiled across the table. "What is it?"

"You know that your parents adopted you when you were just a baby," he said.

She nodded. "Yes. They thought I was special."

"Do you know where you were born?"

She nodded. "In New York. The lady I was born to was a friend of my mom and dad's."

"Right." He considered that a sensitive way for the Weisfields to have put it to her. "There's something very special to me about that."

"What?"

"Your biological mother—the lady you were born to—was my sister."

For a moment, Ashley didn't react, then she asked tentatively. "So…you're my uncle?"

He was worried about her look of concern.

"Yes. Does that make you unhappy?"

"No." That appeared to be a lie. "But…does that mean you can't be my dad?"

So, that was it. Relieved, he drew a breath and reached across the table to touch her arm. "No. I'm still going to adopt you as we planned. But your natural mother was very special to me, and you've been very special to me all along, and now we're sort of connected through her. I like that."

She nodded, happy to believe him but seemingly

unable to absorb what it meant to him. Her bottom line remained. "As long as you can still adopt me."

"Rachel and Erica's uncle is working on it right now."

"Okay." She gathered up her empty cup and plastic spoon to throw them away. "Come on, Brian," she beckoned. "Cartoons are on."

Brian sat on the counter, looking woeful as she skipped away.

Cam, understanding the boy's jealousy, went to hook an arm around him and sweep him off the counter. He turned him upside down until the boy laughed helplessly. He'd like to promise Brian the same future he'd promised Ashley, but he couldn't. The boy still had a mother, such as she was.

He carried him into the living room and dropped him on the sofa beside Ashley, who was already settled in with the remote.

Cam went in search of Mariah, his heart thumping uncomfortably. What if she'd believed that he was telling her to go, instead of understanding that he was simply frustrated by her unwillingness to trust his love for her, trust that it did not have to include biological children?

He concluded a few moments later that she was not in the house. He checked the garage, hoping to find her standing in front of her easel. No such luck.

For a moment, he was distracted by her painting. A boy and a girl Ashley's and Brian's ages ran along the beach, a big black dog in pursuit. A woman trailed after them, her dark hair flying out behind her. In the foreground, a man lying on the sand some distance back from them watched their antics. The tie that connected the four and the dog was somehow palpable.

It was them, he thought. He wished Mariah could have heard Ashley a few minutes ago. She hadn't given a rip about the fact that he and she were related by blood. She just wanted to be sure he could adopt her.

He walked around onto the deck and found it empty. He went the length of it, panic beginning to bubble in his chest, and then, around the far side of the house, he found her on her hands and knees, pulling weeds out of a bed of tomatoes.

Fred stood beside her, looking over her shoulder and occasionally licking her ear. He leaped at Cam when he saw him, tail wagging.

"Hey, Fred."

Mariah cast Cam a glance that said although she was still here, she wasn't happy about it.

"I promised Parker I'd be in her wedding," she explained, "a week from Saturday. And we'll have to see Bart about who takes the children. Just because you declare something to be true doesn't mean that I have to believe it is."

"Obviously," he said, pushing the old bucket she was tossing weeds into nearer to her as she moved down the row. The dog leaned closer to inspect the bucket, but Cam drew him away from it. "You don't believe me when I tell you I love you."

"I believe you," she corrected him. "I just know that feelings can change."

"I thought I was the fortune-teller."

"This isn't a vision. I've seen this phenomenon for myself."

"That wasn't me." He didn't know how to put it any more clearly. "My feelings for you will not change. Except that I don't consider you as smart as I once did."

She didn't answer, just kept weeding the tomatoes. Fred lay down beside her.

Cam went inside to call Hank, since he never had checked in at the office. He was happy to learn that his brief respite was over, and that he'd have to put in a lot of overtime for the rest of this week to keep on schedule.

He stayed away as much as possible for the next four days. When he and Mariah did cross paths, they treated each other with cool politeness in the knowledge that sharp words wouldn't be good for the children. They slept in the same room, but Mariah was usually fast asleep when he came in around midnight, and still asleep when he left before six.

He stayed on his side of the bed, careful not to touch her, unwilling to let her think he was signaling a truce and was willing to capitulate on anything he'd said.

Despite their efforts, he saw that the children were

aware of the antagonism between them and seemed tense themselves. They spent a lot of time in Ashley's room on her computer, Fred at their feet. Cam hated that his argument with Mariah had split their little family into camps.

He slept in Saturday morning, the job finally completed in the wee hours. He was drawn to the kitchen midmorning by a wonderful aroma, and found Mariah serving coffee cake and cocoa to Ashley and Brian, Fred begging between them.

Mariah poured a cup of coffee, set it at his place, then dished up a piece of coffee cake for him. She also pushed the mail toward him.

He took a sip of coffee and looked through the catalogs, junk mail and bills. In the middle of the bills was a legal-size envelope with the seal of the Commonwealth of Massachusetts in the upper left-hand corner.

Assuming it had something to do with the adoption, he slit it open with his butter knife.

He unfolded the one-page letter and read silently.

Dear Mr. and Mrs. Trent,
It has come to the attention of Services to Children and Families that Ashley Weisfield, whom you have filed to adopt, was a twin, and that her brother was given up at birth to a family in Los Angeles. Because of circumstances involving lack of interest and prison time, his family would like to give him up for adoption and

would like to place him with his sister. His name is Brian Barrow. Please contact your attorney and make the necessary arrangements.

Sincerely,
The Governor

Three things were instantly apparent about the letter. First, the paper on which it was printed had been created by copying another letter with the Commonwealth's letterhead and blanking out its contents by placing a clean sheet of paper over it. The line that marked the edge of the sheet was clearly visible.

Second, it had been signed in lavender ink. Ashley was the only one he knew who used lavender ink.

Third, the language had a nonprofessional sound.

Cam was torn between laughter at the effort and anguish that a child's life should come to this—a forged letter pleading for adoption.

He handed Mariah the letter. "You might be interested in this," he said. He looked at the children, one across from him, one on his left, their faces wide-eyed with innocent interest.

"What is it?" Ashley asked.

"You can read it when Mariah's finished," he said. "Would you pass the butter, please?"

Ashley obliged, a stolen glance at Brian the only clue that she was part of the scam.

Mariah turned to Cam, her eyes brimming with tears. For an instant they forgot their animosity in their love and concern for the clever, desperate children who would think up such a scheme. Brian wanted them for a family, and Ashley was lending her skills to help him acquire them.

On the pretext of rereading the letter, Mariah held it up, shielding her face, until she got herself under control.

Then she passed the letter to Ashley, who read it quickly, gasped, passed it on to Brian, then joined him in a well-orchestrated, grandly theatrical round of hugs and grins of surprised delight.

"This is really interesting," Mariah said finally after a deep sip of coffee. "Because I seem to remember that your birthday is in May, Brian, while Ashley's is in December. You've always made a point that you're half a year older than she is."

The children stared, momentarily at a loss. Then Brian said quickly, "That's probably just the date my adopted mother gave me when she took me in."

"I don't think so." Mariah shook her head. "It was listed on the birth certificate in the office at the school."

"Well…" Cam could see the boy's brain at work in his eyes.

"And I don't think the governor gets involved in these kinds of cases."

Brian fell against the back of his chair, busted.

"I told you!" Ashley said, beside herself with exasperation. "I told you! In all my records, the governor's name wasn't mentioned once!"

"It was the purple ink!" Brian shot back at her. "Nobody in the government uses purple ink!"

"You were pretty clever, though," Cam felt obliged to praise. "It was a very artistic approach to the problem. Would have probably landed you in jail if you'd pulled it on anybody else, but, hey. I liked it."

"Cam, you have to find a way to keep me," Brian said, coming to stand beside his chair. "This is the absolute best my life has ever been. Don't let them take me back. Can't we see if your lawyer can work it out so I can stay?"

Cam saw the caution in Mariah's eyes, but he ignored it. "I will," he replied, wrapping his arm around Brian. "I'll talk to him this afternoon."

"Cam," Mariah said under her breath.

A cool glance her way told her to stay out of it.

"What were you doing?" she demanded an hour later. They'd driven the children, showered and clothes changed, to a birthday party at Jackie's house. Now they were on their way home.

"I've been where he is," Cam said calmly. "I know what it's like. I'd have given everything for someone to rescue me."

"But…"

He knew what she was going to say. "I know. You're leaving. But that doesn't mean the court won't let me have him."

"You've been gone fifty hours out of the last sixty-two! How can you raise a child that way?"

"I was avoiding *you,* Mariah," he said with a scolding glance at her. "Hank will adjust my schedule."

"You want us to stay married," she challenged, hurt feelings visible in her eyes, "and you can't stand to be around me."

"I can't stand not to touch you," he corrected her. "Big difference."

She made a sound of exasperation. "Will you please pull over somewhere so we can talk about this?"

He kept driving. "What's to talk about? You've made up your mind."

"I want you to understand," she pleaded, her voice tight and high, "that I sincerely do have your best interest at heart!"

He pulled into a lay-by under the branches of several large maples at the edge of the woods. Once the motor was off, he tore off his seat belt and faced her, one hand on the steering wheel, the other on the back of his seat.

"You want to rip our family apart, leave me to have babies with someone else, and you consider that in my best interest? What is wrong with you?"

"You only want me to stay because you feel sorry for me!" she shouted. "Who wouldn't want to have their own babies if they could?"

"The man who's in love with a woman who *can't* have them!" he roared back at her. "Listen to yourself, Mariah. You're the one with the problem. It isn't…''

His cell phone rang, a weird noise amid the barrage of harsh words. He answered it in the same tone in which he'd been speaking to her. "Hello!"

Then he drew a breath for calm and said on a grim glance at Mariah, "Sorry, Addy. I didn't mean to bark at you. Who's Victorian shower fell in? Oh. Okay. Tell Haley I'll be right there."

He turned off the phone and pulled back out onto the road. "Let's just not talk about it anymore," he said. "You stay for Parker's wedding, and the kids and I'll find a way to get along without you afterward."

In his anger, he was pleased to hear that he sounded as though he could really do that.

CHAPTER SEVENTEEN

CAM WOULD BE JUST FINE without her. Mariah hated that, but reminded herself that whether he believed her or not, she was doing this for him.

He dropped her off at the house, reminded her that she'd have to pick up the children in the middle of the afternoon, then roared away again, headed for Haley and Bart's.

Needing physical activity, Mariah went into a cleaning frenzy, Fred watching but staying a safe distance away. She cleared up the kitchen, cleaned out the refrigerator, then washed the kitchen floor. She emptied the trash, put a new plastic bag in the can, then, with fresh soapy water in the bucket, headed for the bathrooms.

She'd scrubbed one and was about to start on the other one, when she heard the front door open, followed by what sounded like the entire roster of the Chicago Bulls headed her way. Fred ran out to investigate.

Mariah followed just as Ashley thumped past her and into her bedroom. "We're going in-line skating at the Armory!" she shouted from the floor of her

closet. Fred wriggled in beside her, tail wagging.
"Freddy!" she complained, giggling.

"I thought this was a swimming party."

"Yeah, but the pool's closed 'cause something
cracked or something. So Erica's dad brought me
home to get my Rollerblades. Where are they?"

Mariah went to help rummage through the rubble
in the bottom of her closet. She had a shoe rack, but
somehow her shoes never got into it.

Mariah swept everything out.

"There's one!" Ashley said gleefully.

Mariah crawled into the closet, certain the other
must be stuck in a corner.

"Did you know that Cam's my uncle?" Ashley
asked.

On her hands and knees, with pants and coats
brushing her face, Fred kissing her and game or puz-
zle pieces digging into her hands, Mariah stopped
her search, wondering why Cam hadn't mentioned
that he'd told Ashley. Then she remembered that he
couldn't have because they'd barely spoken, except
to shout at each other.

She backed out of the closet to look into Ashley's
face. The little girl had sounded concerned, but she
was turning the wheels on her Rollerblades with
childish distraction.

"You don't like that he's your uncle?" Mariah
asked.

Still fiddling with her Rollerblades, Ashley shook her head. "At first I didn't."

"Why?"

"Because." She put the skate down beside her on the bed and lifted her thin shoulders. "Because I thought if he was my uncle, then they wouldn't let him be my dad. You know. The lawyer or the judge. Whoever decides this stuff."

Mariah wondered if Cam had sufficiently explained their connection.

"Cam is the brother of the woman who gave birth to you, Ashley," she explained gravely. "He's a blood relative."

She didn't seem to get it. "I know," she said, clearly unimpressed, "but he said it's okay 'cause he can still adopt me. I want him to be my dad more than I want him to be my uncle." She smiled, an artless twinkle in her eye. "I've been thinking about you as my mom all year. I still can't believe I made it happen!"

Mariah stared at her, unable to comprehend for a moment that to Ashley, the blood connection meant nothing. Only the fact that Cam still intended to adopt her did.

Ashley held up her Rollerblade. "I need my other one!" she reminded Mariah.

"Right." Mariah shifted mental gears in the interest of Hank, who was waiting in the driveway. On sudden inspiration, she looked under the bed.

Mussed and flushed, she produced the missing skate. Fred barked triumphantly.

Mariah hugged her tightly, then ran for the front door. Mariah followed, catching Fred's collar and waving at Hank as he backed out of the driveway. She felt disoriented, as though she were standing on her head and the view was familiar but not quite right.

Hank stopped and she forced herself to come out of her absorption and display good manners.

Hank leaned out his window to call, "Hey! How's it going?" Then, his eyes narrowing on her face, he asked in concern. "Everything all right?"

"Um…yes. Just got a little frazzled. Ashley was missing one Rollerblade and I didn't want to keep you waiting."

He shrugged that off. "I live with three women and two babies. I wait around a lot. Sorry we had to tear Cam away from you on a Saturday, but the old shower ring fell on Haley while she was shampooing her hair. That old colonial they bought is a disaster, but she loves it. I had a couple of guys buffing up the upstairs bedrooms just so there's a safe place for them and the baby."

"I hope she wasn't hurt when the shower fell."

He grinned. "No. Seems Bart was showering with her. Caught it as it came down." He waggled his eyebrows wickedly. "Now we have something to use against them. Lucky they didn't get stuck. She's pretty big these days.''

Mariah shook her head. "Never a candid camera crew around when you need one.''

Hank laughed and waved again as he backed out of the driveway.

Mariah returned to the house in a mild trance, her conversation with Ashley playing over in her mind. Fred, apparently worn out from the excitement, collapsed in the middle of the floor, coltish legs stretched out.

Once again, she remembered the child's complete lack of reaction to the knowledge that Cam was her uncle, but her obvious delight that the man she'd loved for some time now wanted to take her into his life on a permanent basis.

Blood relationships were important.

Love relationships were everything.

Mariah sat down before the impact of her new perception knocked her down. She felt dizzy, slightly nauseous, sad and happy all at the same time.

This acceptance of a truth she'd denied for so long meant that she had to make some changes in her life. She had to put her babies to rest.

Tears sprang to her eyes as she thought about them—Sarah, who'd survived less than three months in Mariah's womb; Chase, who'd made it to four months; Jane, who'd barely survived two; then

Stephanie, who'd lived almost to birth. Mariah had held her lifeless little body, touching tiny fingers and toes, grieving over her with a pain she could still feel with all its hooks and barbs.

She wiped her tears away and drew a steadying breath. She no longer had room for pain, she told herself as she got to her feet and went to the kitchen table for her car keys. She had a child to raise—maybe two, if things could be made to work in her favor.

And she had a man to love—if it wasn't too late.

She left Fred behind, knowing he would only complicate what she had to do next, then she climbed into her van and drove across town to Maple Hill Mini-Storage, tucked behind an antiques barn. She went to space 27 and dug out her keys.

When she opened the door, she saw the old maple bedroom set that had been her parents and that she and Ben had shared while they were married, and wondered idly if Parker would want it for her new life with Gary.

As an avoidance tactic, she went from item to item, deliberately ignoring the things corralled in the rear corner of the room.

There was the hutch that had been her grandmother's; chairs she'd suspected might be Hepplewhite but that she had yet to check on; a Victorian floor lamp with a gorgeous dragon-shape stand, the shade for it lost long ago. There were boxes of kitchen utensils, books, belongings that had seemed important to save, though there'd been no room for them in her life at the Manor. She'd have to go through them, she thought, and see what she should keep, what Parker might need.

Then, unable to avoid it any longer, reminding herself that this was the reason she'd come, she crossed the empty floor in the middle of the storage space to the collection of baby furniture in the back.

There was everything a new mother might need—the booty from two baby showers and gifts from relatives. A complete nursery in oak decorated with hand-painted ducklings. It had been a present from Ben's parents in their ecstasy over Stephanie's impending arrival. There was a crib, a cradle, a changing table and a bookshelf.

There was the lace-covered bassinet a friend had given her, lavender ribbon woven through the eyelet that covered the white wicker. Beside it were a high chair, a two-speed swing, a car seat and a stroller with all the bells and whistles, which had been a gift from Parker.

In boxes, there were bottles, rattles, toys, blankets and clothing.

As she surveyed the mound now, a sob rose in her throat that she had to swallow away. But she did it. She had too much, she decided, to bemoan what was lost. And the babies would always be with her. Always.

She walked back out to her van to assess space.

As she did, she saw that the spot beside hers was now open and a spiffy white van was pulled up to it. She did a double take when she saw the name painted on the side of it. Evan Braga Painting, part of the Whitcomb's Wonders team.

She was still staring at it when Evan walked out of the dark interior.

He smiled a greeting. "You spring-cleaning, too?" he asked. Then he laughed. "I know it's July, but I'm always a little behind."

"Actually, I'm giving some things to a friend." She laughed. "I was just trying to get an idea of space so that I don't haul out anything that won't fit and have to drag it back in again."

"Can I lend you a hand?" he asked.

That was tempting, but she felt obliged to demur. "Certainly you have better things to do on a Saturday afternoon."

He nodded. "I realize it's pathetic, but I haven't. I'll be happy to help. If we fill both vans, maybe we can make it in one trip. Show me what's going."

She brought him inside and indicated the baby things.

Everyone knew she and Cam were adopting Ashley, and she wouldn't be surprised—given Rita Robidoux's informal information center and Addy Whitcomb's commitment to anyone who needed it—if everyone didn't also know about her divorce and the reason for it.

"All of it?" he asked, surveying the stack.

"All of it," she replied. "I...I have another life now."

He gave her a sympathetic smile. "Me, too. And to get it, I had to part with a lot of things that were grafted onto me. At least, that's how it seemed when I had to leave them."

She felt the comfort offered in his admission and thanked him with an answering smile.

"All right," he said briskly. "You have a seat in your van and I'll pack everything."

"I'll help with the smaller stuff," she insisted.

"Why not." He hefted the crib, still in its original box. "Cam says there's little point in arguing with you."

She followed him out to the van with a clown lamp in one hand and a giant teddy bear in the other, sure Cam hadn't meant that in a good way.

CAM STRADDLED THE EDGES of Haley and Bart's ball-and-claw tub while he reconnected the shower ring to the ceiling supports. He'd already repaired the faucet, which had ripped a few threads when the ring fell, and reconnected the back part of the ring, and was applying the last few turns of a wrench to the front.

Haley sat on the closed lid of the john, kibitzing.

She'd taken one look at him when he'd arrived, given him a cup of coffee with something in it he wasn't supposed to have while on the job, then wheedled out of him the reason he looked like someone condemned to die.

He'd tried to explain briefly, only because she was feeling guilty, sure he appeared so grim because she'd dragged him away from his family on a Saturday. But she hadn't been satisfied with a brief explanation and had demanded details.

"So, she has been unreasonable and mistrustful," she said of Mariah. "But women aren't rational about their children. And I'm trying to imagine how I would feel if I woke up tomorrow and realized the baby I was carrying was no longer alive. I'd...I'd want to die myself! And if it had happened after three other miscarriages, well..." Her eyes welled with tears.

"Haley..." He wanted to sidetrack her. Bart had told him she'd been emotional and weepy.

But she was determined. "Cam, it's not an even playing field," she said urgently. "You have to try to understand her. If Bart left me because I couldn't give him a child after all I'd been through in the attempt—"

"What is going on?" Bart demanded. He walked into the bathroom, a cordless phone in his hand, a frown on his face as he glanced from Haley's tear-filled eyes to the weary misery in Cam's.

"We were talking about babies dying and husbands leaving," she said, giving the roll of toilet tissue a slap and ripping off a length to dry her eyes. "I'm trying to help him with Mariah."

"Maybe it would be a good idea to talk about more positive things," Bart proposed.

"Those are her problems," Haley insisted on a sniffle. "We've dealt with our dragons and want the world to be sunny and bright, but she's still dealing with hers. And the death of babies...my God. It isn't fair to expect her to see things from our positive points of view."

Cam held on to the shower ring as he viewed Mariah's attitude from a new perspective. Because he hadn't had much in the way of love and security from the beginning of his life, he'd been able to take most of his disappointments—including his marriage—with a certain philosophical steadiness.

Mariah, however, had loved Ben, thought she had the perfect situation, then lost everything. That had to be worse.

He heard himself tell her to leave, that he'd cope without her, and wished desperately that he could take back the words. He felt morose—and mean.

"If anyone says one more thing to me about death or divorce, I will leave the two of you to your miseries and eat my jambalaya all by myself," Bart threatened.

Haley grabbed his arm and used it to lever herself

to her feet. "There's no need to get nasty," she said, wrapping her arms around him. Because of her bulky tummy, she made it only halfway. "I was just trying to do a little marriage counseling. Poor Cam looks like death." At the sound of the word, she quickly put a hand over her mouth. "That was involuntary," she said.

Bart pointed her out of the room. "Go sit with your feet up and think cheerful thoughts. Think about the baby shower your mom can finally give you now that we have space to put things."

She smiled at Cam as she backed out of the room. "It never hurts to try one more time. If Bart hadn't been patient with me, I'd be someone else's problem now."

Bart shook his head wryly. "If only I'd known then..."

"You'd have loved me anyway!" she shouted after she disappeared.

Cam tested the ring for steadiness. The back wobbled slightly. He turned and walked gingerly back toward it to tighten the connection.

"About Brian," Bart said, leaning against the pedestal sink.

Cam stopped, wrench to the joint. "Yeah?"

"I just spoke to his mother."

Cam was shocked. He'd mentioned to Bart when he'd first arrived today that he'd like to talk to him about obtaining temporary custody of Brian, but he hadn't expected Bart to get right on it. And he hadn't expected him to be able to reach Anjanette Barrow.

"And?" he asked.

"One of the people she hit is paralyzed. She's going to jail for a while. She's open to the idea. She wants to speak to her lawyer about it."

Cam tried to remember that he was straddling a small chasm. "You're kidding!"

"I'm not. I'm sure we can make it work. He'll want to have a look at you, of course, but what's not to like? And it'll be easy to get testimonials from the Lightfoot sisters."

"I can't believe it."

Bart grinned. "Brian will be thrilled. Seems to think the world of you, no matter how hard I try to straighten him out."

Haley appeared in the doorway again. "Mariah's here with Evan," she announced, looking surprised.

"Evan?" Cam asked. Had Mariah replaced him already?

"Yeah. He pulled up right behind her."

The doorbell pealed as they spoke.

"You'd better hurry out there, mister," Haley said to Cam. "Evan's a cutie. Don't want to let her develop any ideas."

Cam got off the tub and followed Haley and Bart to the living room. Haley opened the door and Evan walked in carrying a large box with Crib stenciled on it. "Where do you want this?" he asked.

"I didn't order…" Haley began, but Mariah led the way around her, pushing a stroller bearing a lamp with a clown base.

"I have all this…stuff," Mariah said, her voice a little choked despite her sincere, if fragile smile. "I can't use it, and I thought of you."

She steered the stroller around the corner and almost collided with Cam. She stopped. The look in her eyes was clear—clearer than he'd ever seen it—except for a peripheral pain she appeared determined to ignore. She seemed curiously unburdened.

"Hi," she said with a hesitant but affectionate smile. "How's the shower ring going?"

He wondered if he was delusional. "Almost finished," he replied. "What's all this?"

She expelled a breath. "The contents of my storage locker. We're not going to need it. There's lots more stuff, if you wouldn't mind helping. Poor Evan put most of it in the vans."

The contents of her storage locker. It seemed to symbolize the babies she'd never quite been able to give up. She must have found a way to deal with them. What had happened while he'd been gone?

And…*we're* not going to need it?

"Here." Evan handed him the large box. "We'll form a brigade. I'll carry in and hand off to Bart, who'll carry to you. While we're working, the women will make us refreshments.''

Bart appeared with a rocking chair. "Haley's in no condition to be trusted with fire. She's running around like an insane person, looking into the van windows and weeping.''

"Evan, you push the stroller," Mariah advised, skinnying by them in the hallway. "I'll get coffee going and see what I can find for refreshments.''

Evan scratched his head. "I had such a good plan and already we have a bottleneck.''

The things were moved in and carried upstairs in half an hour. One bedroom, smelling of fresh paint and floor wax, was set up with the baby furniture, and another was filled with toys and other paraphernalia.

Haley couldn't stop crying.

Bart finally wrapped his arms around her and rubbed her back. "Honey, you have to calm down," he advised gently. "You're going to make yourself sick.''

Haley shook her head. "I'm fine, and I'm thrilled. But it touches me to know that this represents all Mariah's hopes and dreams and…she's given it to us!''

Needing desperately to touch Mariah, to hold her, Cam smiled at Bart over the top of Haley's head. "Excuse Mariah and me if we don't stay. We've got to…''

"Go," Bart said, apparently not requiring an explanation.

Evan caught Cam's arm as he walked past him. "Lots of people start over," he said quietly, "but not all of them have to do it by ripping out the old life. That hurts. You gotta respect those who can do that."

Cam nodded. "I know." He hadn't a clue how that nugget of wisdom related to Evan's life, but he understood what it meant in Mariah's.

He ran down the stairs and into the kitchen, where Mariah stood on a step stool, rooting through a cupboard for something.

MARIAH'S HANDS WERE TREMBLING as she searched through the cupboards for sugar for the coffee and some small treat to go with it.

Cam hadn't looked entirely pleased to see her. Not that she'd expected him to be—except in her wildest dreams involving forgiveness or, at least, loss of memory.

She turned at the sound of footsteps in the kitchen and saw him walking toward her. Her perch gave her a slight height advantage over him.

"I want to talk to you," he said, as a demand rather than a suggestion. He was apparently unaware of *any* advantage on her part. Still, it was better than the "I never want to see you again!" she thought might be on his tongue.

"Let me just finish..." she began, pointing to the coffee dripping into the steamy carafe.

"Sorry." He wrapped an arm around her hips and scooped her off the stool. "Can't wait that long."

"Cam!" she squealed, holding on with both arms around his neck as he strode toward the door, tipped her sideways as he went through it, then put her on her feet beside his truck, which was parked on the street.

Neighbors working on their lawns paused to stare.

"Where are we going?" she asked.

"Home," he replied, opening the passenger door and leaning on it as he looked into her eyes. His were dark and purposeful. "If you have a problem with that, speak now."

Her answer was to climb into the truck.

He locked and closed the door, then drove home. He didn't say a word while he pulled into the driveway, parked and came around to open her door.

He was trying to find a diplomatic way to tell her it was over, she thought, feeling panicky. Her epiphany had come too late. He'd probably brought her home to get her things.

He led her around the house onto the deck, to the pair of wicker chairs they'd bought at a rummage sale. She'd made bright flowered cushions for them— She had a sudden, overwhelming realization of all she was about to lose.

From inside the house, Fred barked a question.

No one ever returned from a trip to town and went out onto the deck without first releasing him to join them.

Cam put her into one of the chairs, then turned his back to the lake and leaned against the railing.

"You gave away all your baby things," he observed quietly.

She nodded, her throat tightening. "I finally realized that I have to act on what I have now, rather than what I lost then." She hitched a shoulder, the pain persisting despite her new understanding. "Hank brought Ashley home to pick up her Rollerblades and she told me you explained about being her uncle. I thought she was upset about it, but it was only because she thought that meant you couldn't be her dad." A tear slid down her cheek. "I finally got it. A year ago, I'd have been happy to die with Stephanie. Today, I really want to be Ashley's mother." She held Cam's gaze, emotion burning her throat. "I want to stay here with you and be your wife for a long, long time."

That was everything he wanted to hear. He caught her hand to pull her out of the chair and wrapped her in his arms. He held her close as she kissed his neck.

"I love you," she said tearfully. "I do. But to admit that to myself, I had to put my babies away and that was hard." She kissed his cheeks. "Can you understand that?"

"Of course. I don't expect you to forget them—just to make room for me and Ashley." He looked into her eyes. "And while you're doing that, you'd better make room for Brian, because Bart seems to think we're going to get him."

He explained about the jail sentence and Brian's mother's willingness to give them temporary custody of the boy. He grinned. "So, according to your message from the future," he said, assuming his son of Othar accent, his arms looped around her, his hands joined at her back, "we have to get a swing set, paint Fred yellow and visit the capitals of Europe."

Her expression was almost rapturous. And he felt everything reflected in her eyes and her smile. He could hardly believe this was his life.

The sound of a motor in the driveway was followed almost instantly by childish shouts of "Cam! Mariah!" There was pounding on the front door.

"We're out here!" Cam shouted.

Fred, standing at the living room window, barked furiously.

The children thundered toward them, Hank following more slowly.

"Guess what?" Ashley asked breathlessly, her eyes enormous.

Before Cam or Mariah could try, Brian said, beside himself with excitement, "They found the gold!"

For a minute, Cam didn't know what he was talking about. Then he remembered. "The gold the Confederate stole?"

"Yeah! Some of my men were working on the ceiling in Mariah's old room—"

"They had to take off all the plaster and wood and when they got to the...you know...the wood stuff—"

"The beams! They found an old bank bag tied to the beam with a belt!"

The children talked over each other, almost levitating in their excitement.

Cam looked up at Hank, unable to believe they had the facts straight.

Hank confirmed it with a nod. "My guys called me. Do you believe it? I dropped by with the kids to see it on our way home. Brian's going to get his picture taken with it, too, since he looked so hard for it, according to Letitia. Got to go. Just wanted to make sure you were here."

"Thanks, Hank!" Mariah called as he walked away. He waved as he rounded the corner.

Cam put a hand to Brian's shoulder. "I'll bet you're pretty disappointed you're not the one who found it."

Brian smiled. It didn't seem to be the case. "That was just so me and Ashley could go to Disneyland. But who cares about that."

Now that the children had joined them, Fred was

apoplectic. But Cam wanted to make sure Mariah caught the full import of this.

"You don't want to go to Disneyland anymore?" Cam asked.

"Well, yeah," Brian replied. "Someday when we can all go. But so far, this summer's been the *best* right here."

"How come Fred's inside?" Ashley asked, frowning at the dog, who was all but standing on his head for attention. "Can I go get him?"

"Sure," Mariah replied. "Bring a couple of colas and the tin of brownies."

The children pushed each other toward the back door and exploded into the house, the dog barking and leaping at them.

"Did you hear that?" Cam asked Mariah, leaning down to kiss her gently.

"Means we have to go to Disneyland before we go to Europe," she said.

She squeezed him with surprising strength in someone so small. Love, he knew, was empowering.

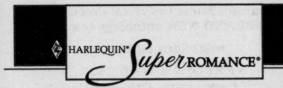

HARLEQUIN *Super*ROMANCE®

They'd grown up at Serenity House—a group home
for teenage girls in trouble. Now Paige, Darcy and
Annabelle are coming back for a special reunion,
and each has her own story to tell.

SERENITY HOUSE

An exciting new trilogy
by
Kathryn Shay

Practice Makes Perfect—June 2002
A Place to Belong—Winter 2003
Against All Odds—Spring 2003

Available wherever Harlequin books are sold.

HARLEQUIN®
Makes any time special®

C'mon back home to Crystal Creek with a BRAND-NEW anthology from

bestselling authors

Vicki Lewis Thompson
Cathy Gillen Thacker
Bethany Campbell

Return to Crystal Creek

Nothing much has changed in Crystal Creek... till now!

The mysterious Nick Belyle has shown up in town, and what he's up to is anyone's guess. But one thing is certain. Something big is going down in Crystal Creek, and folks aren't going to rest till they find out what the future holds.

Look for this exciting anthology, on-sale in July 2002.

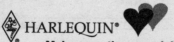

These New York Times *bestselling authors*
have created stories to capture the hearts and minds
of women everywhere.
Here are three classic tales about the power of love—
and the wonder of discovering the place
where you belong....

FINDING HOME

DUNCAN'S BRIDE
by
LINDA HOWARD

CHAIN LIGHTNING
by
ELIZABETH LOWELL

POPCORN AND KISSES
by
KASEY MICHAELS

Available only from Silhouette
at your favorite retail outlet.

Where love comes alive™